THE JANITOR AND THE SPY

The Thornhill Series

Book I

S W ELLENWOOD

ISBN: 1508902992
ISBN 13: 9781508902997
Library of Congress Control Number: 2015904314
CreateSpace Independent Pub. Platform
North Charleston, South Carolina

To you, my first reader. Thanks for taking a chance on me.

CHAPTER 1

BLOOD AND BABY WIPES

Thomas Thornhill sat in the restroom stall of the Rosa Parks Transit Center in Detroit, Michigan, wiping blood and ash from his hands with a baby wipe. He took the last two wipes from the pouch and cleaned the blood off his wrists and the dirt off his dress shoes. He put the wipes in his suit pocket and opened his small suitcase, moving the bagged Walther PPK/S pistol off a set of clothes.

The restroom door opened.

Thornhill froze and then quietly lifted his feet off the floor. He slowly pulled a knife out of his dinner jacket and held it ready. He heard the sound of urinating across from his stall, a flush, and then footsteps going out of the bathroom. Thornhill grimaced over the fact that he'd heard no water running in the sink. However, the other man's lack of hygiene did not deter him from his mission.

He quickly pulled out the bag of clothes, which contained a dark-blue polo shirt and a pair of slim-fit khaki pants. A pair of Vans, also bagged, that matched his new outfit sat at the bottom of the suitcase with a pair of black dress shoes and a custom-tailored dinner suit.

As Thornhill changed out of his dirty suit and into his new outfit, he pondered how he had ended up in this predicament. Had it begun at birth? Was it because of the absence of a real home? The lack of close friends during middle school? High school crushes? Graduating early? Interning at the NSA? Sparring with the military police? His parents' deaths? Saying yes to Crumwell? They had all played a part, but it was when he'd deplaned in Amsterdam that it had all gone south.

How foolish he'd been to think it would be an easy mission.

CHAPTER 2

A Child's Curiosity

It was early morning in Schiphol, Amsterdam, when Thornhill's flight touched down at the airport. He had barely woken up when they started to descend, giving him just enough time to check whether his suitcase, stowed underneath his seat, was still secure. It contained polos, khakis, two suits, and a tablet connected to the Silence network. The single black thread woven through the suitcase's zipper was still intact, which brought a smile to Thornhill's face. He put on his tan suit coat and finished folding up his blanket just as the aircraft touched down. After several minutes of taxiing, the plane reached the gate. Thornhill turned on his smartphone and put in his earpiece.

"Good morning, Mr. Smith. I hope you had a good flight," said Mallory McArthur, Thornhill's handler.

Thornhill pulled his luggage out from under his seat and waited for some of the other first-class passengers to exit the plane. "It was indeed. Thank you for the advice about getting ahead of the jet lag. It's working wonderfully so far," he said, bidding the flight attendant farewell with a nod.

"I am glad to hear it," said Mallory. "You have appointments with clients at one and four today. Jones is waiting for you at Departure One."

"Good. I won't be able to get the one o'clock, but I'll make the four o'clock. Please send him my apologies." Thornhill exited his gate and headed toward the passport control center.

"I will. Call me if you have any questions."

"I will. Good-bye." Thornhill ended the call and casually walked toward the passport control center, making his way through the crowd, which ranged from businesspeople to families of tourists. With his outfit and suitcase, he looked like a typical international businessman. He reached customs in no time and waited in line behind a family with four kids, ranging in age from nine months to thirteen years.

The father was an average-looking man, wearing khaki shorts and white socks that had matched the color of his shoes when the shoes were new. He told his kids to hand the officer their passports. They followed his instructions well, handing their passports to the officer one at a time. The hard part was keeping them still and quiet. They were unable to contain their excitement at being in a new place with new sights and new smells.

The mother waited on the other side of security, nursing her nine-month-old baby while many passing travelers looked at her with disgust. It seemed to make no difference to her. Five minutes later, the father finally got the rest of his family through customs, dragging away one of the boys, who couldn't stop asking the officer questions about his job.

"Passport?" the officer asked Thornhill with a chuckle in his voice as the family slowly made their way to the baggage claim.

"A funny bunch," commented Thornhill as he handed the officer his fake passport.

"They are indeed," said the officer as he looked over the document, comparing the picture on it to Thornhill. The faces were the same: short, thick brown hair, brown eyes under thin eyebrows, an oval head with small ears, an average face. All the legal stamps and information needed were present. The officer stamped the passport, handed it back to Thornhill, and said, "Welcome to Amsterdam."

"Thank you," said Thornhill, taking his passport and heading to Departure One. He quickly passed the family, the parents still trying to corral their kids, before heading out. Thornhill spied a man in a chauffeur's uniform who was holding a sign with John Smith on it. He was of average height, with short blond hair and dark-green eyes in a clean-shaven face.

"Mr. Smith?" he inquired as Thornhill approached.

"I take it you are my ride?" asked Thornhill.

"John Jones, sir. I will if you let me, dear sir."

Thornhill felt a sense of relief flow through him. Jones's response was the all-clear phrase.

Jones left to bring the car around. Thornhill looked around at the hundreds of civilians coming and going from the Amsterdam airport. Among them, he caught a glimpse of the eldest son of the family he'd seen earlier, a thin nine-year-old boy with blue eyes and a Batman shirt. He was looking straight at Thornhill. Thornhill imagined the little boy walking up and asking him in a soft whisper, "Are you a spy?" Thornhill chuckled a little on the inside at the thought of it.

Jones drove the car up and opened the door for him. Thornhill took his seat in the back, full of excitement and energy as his first spy mission began…not knowing it would also be his last.

CHAPTER 3

THE COST OF A LIFE

Thornhill got into the car, a black BMW, as Jones put his luggage in the trunk. Once in the car, Jones gave Thornhill a small nod in the rearview mirror and drove off.

Thornhill turned on his tablet and connected to the Silence network. The FBI, CIA, and NSA logos all appeared on a dull-blue screen divided by three diagonal lines that met in the middle. Thornhill pressed the small triangle created by the merging lines in the middle of the screen. The logos vanished off to the sides, leaving the blue screen empty. Thornhill placed his hand on the screen. The tablet scanned his hand and then the tablet's camera scanned his face. The screen changed to bright green. Removing his hand, Thornhill saw that the word "Glass" had appeared, accompanied by a female voice saying, "Welcome, Agent Thornhill." The word was then replaced by his handler's face, a change for the better, in Thornhill's opinion.

"Glad to see you made it to the car safely," said Mallory. The blond, blue-eyed woman was wearing a light-blue button-down shirt with the sleeves rolled up.

"Worried that I would get kidnapped by terrorists? Mallory, I didn't know you cared that much."

"No, I was afraid that you would get lost."

"Your faith in me is overwhelming."

Mallory's mouth betrayed a glimmer of a smile. "What faith?"

"Ouch," said Thornhill as he placed his hand on his heart. Jones snickered.

"Now, can we get down to business?" asked Mallory.

"Of course. What am I here for?"

"In 1939, Armend and Emmalina Golay moved to America from Switzerland—same old story, seeking the American dream. Two years later, they had a son named Nils Willermus Golay." The tablet showed an old picture of the Golay family in front of their general store in Pennsylvania: an average-looking immigrant family, dark-haired father, blond mother, and a child in the middle with large ears for a boy his age. "The Golays lived in the states until the father died of cancer in '61. The mother returned to Switzerland with her son a year later."

"Sad story. I would like hear more. However, I would also like to know how this is related to the security of America or the communication channels between bureaus," said Thornhill.

Just then, Jones merged onto the A4 highway toward Amsterdam, getting behind a pink Fiat. As they passed the car, Thornhill did a double take to make sure it wasn't just a trick of the light. It wasn't. It was a pink Fiat.

"Well, until two days ago," Mallory continued, "Nils Golay was completely off the radar. Disappeared around '68 until now when we received a letter from Golay claiming he was part of a covert anticommunist branch of the NSA and had been sent to Switzerland to monitor the flow of large sums of money that could potentially be used to support communist groups across the world. Several years later, he received a letter claiming his division had been liquidated."

"He sent us a letter? Like snail mail?" asked Thornhill.

A scanned picture of the letter Golay received some forty-odd years ago and the letter Golay sent two days ago came up on Thornhill's tablet.

"Does his story check out?" asked Thornhill.

Mallory grimaced. "Somewhat."

Thornhill pressed his lips together and furrowed his brow. "Somewhat? Where does it fall short?"

"I couldn't find any records of his employment with the NSA, but I did find that, starting a few weeks before he left for Switzerland and until two months after flying there, he was in the process of buying a house, and yet his account still had the same amount in it as it did a couple of weeks before he left. And no bank loans were taken out in his name."

"So, the NSA could have paid him for the travel and housing. In return for what? What was his cover?" Thornhill's curiosity was growing.

Mallory continued. "He was a managerial assistant at one of the largest banks in Switzerland until his disappearance. He showed no signs of activity till now."

Thornhill nodded as he read over the letter Nils Golay had sent to Glass. "So who was the letter addressed to? He's using pronouns." The letter was handwritten and asked the reader to meet Golay at the Rusland, an Amsterdam coffee shop, at eleven the next day.

"They didn't give me that information, but I suspect someone high up, someone that knew him," responded Mallory.

"Interesting." Thornhill swiped through pictures of the coffee shop where he would be meeting Golay. The walls were a dark red except the one behind the counter, which was covered by a huge, black chalkboard, one that Thornhill would have loved as a kid. The rest of the room was set up like an ordinary coffee shop: small four-chair tables littered the main floor, and there were pairs of black leather arm-chairs in the corners and at the back. "So, all I need to do is talk with him and see what's up?"

"That's it," said Mallory, nodding, her ponytail swinging slightly.

"Then why is Jones my support?" asked Thornhill in bewilderment, looking at Jones in the rearview mirror. "I could understand sending another young agent, like Oaks or

Westfall, but a former marine sniper? Little overkill." Jones chuckled. "See, he agrees with me," said Thornhill.

"I didn't assign the agents. I'm just the handler. I would take it as a sign to not take this mission lightheartedly." There was a hint of worry in Mallory's voice. "He will cover you from a lookout point across the street." A 3-D map of the street came up on the tablet, showing the precise position Jones would have. A small construction site on an adjoining street, coupled with the coffee shop's wall-sized windows, gave Jones a perfect view of the coffeehouse's interior and exterior. "You will also be armed."

Thornhill frowned. "With what?"

Jones reached into a compartment between the driver's and passenger's seats, pulled out a black handgun, and handed it to Thornhill. It seemed to absorb the light hitting it; there was no reflection or gloss on it.

"A regular Glock nine millimeter with optional silencer, one of the most common handguns in Europe," said Mallory. "We retrieved it from a stash of confiscated guns in France, no strings. What makes it different is the bullets."

Thornhill took out the clip to study one of the bullets. The tip of the bullet wasn't rounded like a dome, but pointed. "Armor-piercing rounds?"

"Indeed. Each bullet costs about three hundred American dollars."

Thornhill's eyes widened as he whistled. "Glad to know how much a life costs." He carefully placed the bullet back in the clip, hoping he wouldn't have to use it.

"We're here," said Jones as they pulled up to the Mauro Mansion hotel.

"You will be meeting Golay at the Rusland coffee shop at eleven tomorrow," Mallory said. "We will use your smaller earpiece to keep in touch and record the conversation for analyzing and training purposes. You and Jones will log in to Silence at ten twenty tomorrow via earpiece, understood?"

"Understood."

"Good. Ending session. Be safe." The tablet went black, and a young valet with red hair and blue eyes opened the car door and said in Dutch, "Welcome to the Mauro Mansion."

CHAPTER 4

COLD FRIENDS

Thornhill was already awake when his alarm went off at 7:30 a.m. He lifted himself off the soft bed and turned off the alarm clock on the nightstand beside him. A hammock chair hung from the ceiling between the bed and the window overlooking the river. Thornhill got up and opened the window. The sun reflected off the river and onto the tightly packed buildings on the far side. Reflections created waves of light upon the buildings like waves upon the beach.

He took a deep breath of Amsterdam, a city of the young and old, where the past sat down with the future and talked about the present at the riverside, where travelers passed through on a journey toward the older and newer cities of Europe or stayed to fulfill their fleshly desires in secret. Thornhill exhaled air back into the city, a breath not as mysterious as the city itself, though that would change.

He closed the window, walked over to the phone, and called room service to order *uitsmijter*, a fried egg-and-ham breakfast with white toast, and an orange juice, pulp-free. He then proceeded to do a quick morning workout, focusing on his cardio more than anything else. When he finished at eight o'clock, he took a shower.

He quickly cleaned his body, the average-looking body of a healthy man, a body that gave no hint that it had gone through marine physical training with flying colors, unofficially besting the record time at the hardest marine obstacle course in the world. Once done showering, he took a minute to just stand under the water, playing through the day in his head. What should he be eating when Golay came in? What should he say, and what would Golay's response be? His thoughts were cut short when he heard a knock at the door and a young woman's voice saying "Room service!" in Dutch.

"Just a moment," he shouted back in Dutch. Quickly turning off the shower, he got out, wrapped a towel around his waist, and went to the door. Opening the door revealed a young maid, black hair in a tight bun to one side of her thin, pale face. The only color she sported was dull-red lipstick and pink blush, which seemed to brighten when she saw Thornhill.

"Sorry to bother you, sir, but here is your uitsmijter," said the maid, avoiding eye contact as she handed him his breakfast tray.

"It's all right. Thank you." Thornhill took his hands off the door and his towel to take his meal. However, he'd failed to fix his towel around his waist properly, and he felt it slipping quickly down his legs. He shoved his hip against the open doorframe to keep his towel up as he tried to use his other foot to close the door. "Give me a moment and I'll give you a tip," he said.

Unfortunately, his maneuvering failed to hold up the towel, and he was exposed. The maid clearly could not stop herself from smiling while Thornhill regained his composure. She quickly turned and walked away with her cart, almost jogging, quietly chuckling her way down the hall. Thornhill pulled his towel in with his foot and closed the door with his hip. Once inside, he stood still for a minute, looking at his food and then his naked self in the mirror.

"Smooth moves. Bond would be proud," Thornhill said to himself as he put the tray on his bed and started to get dressed. "Beautiful start to your first mission," he added while putting on his black boxer briefs. "A beautiful woman brings you breakfast and catches you, literally, with your pants down." He sat down on his bed with his uitsmijter and turned on his tablet to watch the news. "It would have been worse if it had been an assassin. Gosh, Mallory wouldn't like that."

Thornhill started to eat and pushed the event to the back of his mind. While he ate, an anchorman talked of stocks. A couple of minutes passed, and the news changed to a special about a Triad family called Wu. At that point, Thornhill gave a loud chuckle at the entire situation and the maid's reaction.

Once he was done with his meal, he got dressed. His suit was a dark blue and an English cut, tailored to conceal certain items from the public's eye. His silver tie gave his whole appearance a modern, angular look. Fully dressed, he went downstairs, where Jones was already waiting for him by the car, dressed as he'd been the day before.

"Don't forget to check your e-mail," said Jones as he sat down in the driver's seat. Thornhill pulled out his tablet, wondering what he could have missed. He signed in and checked his mail. Nothing new. Just then, he got a video call, not from his handler, but from the director of Glass himself, Mr. Crumwell, a thin old man with scant white hair and blue eyes that glared through rimless reading glasses. Crumwell's hands shook slightly from Parkinson's as he moved papers around on his desk.

"Good afternoon. I hope you are having a good day so far," said Crumwell.

"I've had an interesting morning, sir," answered Thornhill.

"I hope nothing threatening."

Thornhill chuckled. "No, sir. Just an awkward situation. I believe it will give you a good laugh in my report."

Crumwell gave a smile, the one he usually tossed out when he was confused about something. "That is actually why I am calling," he said as his smile faded. "You and Jones will not be required to write a report for this mission." Crumwell took his glasses off, his left hand shaking. "Because this mission will not be on record."

"Understood," responded Thornhill. "Does my handler know?"

"Yes. However, I wanted to inform you of this matter personally."

Thornhill nodded. "Understood."

"This doesn't change anything about the mission, except secrecy is your top priority, even before the safety of yourself or your fellow team members."

In his peripheral vision, Thornhill caught Jones looking back at him. But Thornhill didn't break eye contact with Crumwell.

"Any questions?" the director asked.

"Besides my handler, Jones, and myself, who else knows?"

"No one."

Thornhill nodded and asked the bigger question on his mind. "Sir, who was the letter sent to?" He asked this though he already had a good sense of who it was.

Crumwell kept his face blank and said nothing. Thornhill raised an eyebrow and asked, "A friend from the Cold War?"

"Yes. I will fill you in later, after you talk to Golay. And remember, Thornhill"—Crumwell's glasses shook in his hands—"play the part."

The screen went black. Thornhill put the tablet in the pocket behind the driver's seat and sat in silence, thinking about how this, his first mission, would also been an off-the-books mission. Why was this mission being kept a secret, though?

Jones broke the silence. "Looks like a simple mission, even off the books."

"Yeah, however, it does raise the question, why so secret? What kind of information does this guy have to force Crumwell to keep it off the books?" Thornhill observed the outside world as he pondered this question.

Jones shrugged before asking, "Just to know who I'm working with, since we haven't worked together before, do you flirt well?"

Thornhill shrugged as well. "Decent enough for a spy. I try to work on it as much as I can. Though it does get me in trouble every so often."

Jones chuckled and responded, "Good, because that is not my strong suit. I'm better at just blending in."

"Hey, whatever gets the mission done, that's good enough. Crumwell always told me that to be a great spy, all you need is two abilities: being able to figure out what mask to wear to complete the mission and wearing that mask like it was your own flesh." Jones nodded, and Thornhill thought about the masks he would wear during this mission. His musings stopped abruptly as Jones turned the corner and they reached their destination.

CHAPTER 5

UNEXPECTED GUESTS

Thornhill ordered a white chocolate mocha, a tomato sandwich, and an espresso. He sat down two tables away from the front door. In black leather chairs behind him near the back wall sat a young couple, possibly on a first date based on how the man acted toward the woman, leaning forward, hanging on every word she spoke, gazing into her eyes as if they were a morning sunrise. Sadly, she didn't seem to notice. A middle-aged man sat midway between Thornhill and the couple. He had a large coffee cup, a couple of books, and a notepad. His gray hair came down to his shoulders, falling past brown glasses over brown eyes. A redheaded barista checked her phone behind the counter. No one else was in the coffee shop.

Thornhill started to read a copy of *Harriet the Spy*, as the letter had instructed. Jones would already be in position at the construction site a block down the connecting road, giving him a perfect view, through the scope of his Blaser R93, of the coffee shop and the stores next to it.

"Everyone in position?" asked Mallory over the communicators. Thornhill wiped the side of his nose with his right pointer finger as if something was on it.

"The agent and I are in position," reported Jones over the communicator. "Is the line secured?"

"No jammers or interceptors on the map," said Mallory. "Even if there was one, it would have to be from the future to intercept this transmission."

"Glad to hear," replied Jones.

"How many people in the room with Thornhill?"

"Four. The employee is on her phone, and there's an old man two tables behind Thornhill and a young couple in the back. None armed."

"Good," said Mallory, "already on the cell phone and tracking it."

"Any possible threats?"

"None. The girl is just looking up stuff about that new pop star, Justin Gribber."

"So, you're saying I should shoot her?"

Mallory laughed. Thornhill gave a small chuckle under his breath.

"Red light on that, sadly," said Mallory. "Thirty minutes till—"

"He's here," said Jones, cutting her off. A man who appeared to be in his seventies and who matched the pictures of Golay came walking up to the coffee shop from the left side of the street. He stood about five foot five and probably weighed less than a hundred and forty pounds. He was balding, with snow-white hair and a thin, clean-shaven face. He wore an old, black, sixties-style suit, a blue tie, and gold cufflinks. He entered the Rusland carrying only a brown leather messenger bag.

Thornhill heard Golay give a quiet sigh as he came in, as if he was remembering something. He could tell the man hadn't been in the field in a long time. Golay walked over, sat down in the chair across from Thornhill, and slowly placed his bag under his chair. Mallory and Jones kept silent, ready with any information—or bullets—Thornhill needed.

"Hello, Mr. Golay, nice to meet you," said Thornhill, extending his hand for a handshake. Golay accepted it. "I hope you enjoy espresso," said Thornhill. Then he waited for the correct response.

"I do. The liquid gold of beans, some say. Thank you," responded Golay. Thornhill caught a sigh of relief from Mallory. Golay had a Germanic accent, but his English was fluent.

Golay took a sip of his espresso and then took a deep breath and said, "Just as I remember." Thornhill knew that would send Mallory into a flurry of activity to find out when and why Golay was last in Amsterdam.

"Glad to hear. So…" Thornhill closed his book and set it on the table. He crossed his legs, placed his hands on them, and asked, "What do you want to talk about?"

Golay took another sip of his coffee in a dreamy way. "I'm old," he said.

"He could have traveled to Amsterdam in '68 after his mother died. A couple of possible NSA aliases traveled from Switzerland to Amsterdam that year," Mallory informed Thornhill.

Golay sighed again. "I am still surprised I have lived this long, with what I know. Not saying that I regret it, not at all. My life has had its ups." He paused. "And downs. Though I hold that not to bad luck, but time. Even the cat runs out of lives when he's too curious."

"What was the cat curious about? Communism?" asked Thornhill.

Golay snorted. "I wish it was that simple."

"Thornhill," said Jones, "three men in baggy shorts are coming your way from my direction. They're armed."

Thornhill could see them slowly walking toward him on the other side of the street. A tall black man with sunglasses, wearing an FC Barcelona jersey a size too big, walked between two shorter Caucasian men; one wore a gray hoodie, which obscured his face, while the other was clad in a black stocking cap and a long-sleeved Miami Heat shirt.

"Can you get anything on them, Mallory?" asked Jones.

"Working on it now," replied Mallory.

"You see, my story is a long and sad one," Golay continued. Thornhill kept his ears on Golay and his eyes on the three men approaching the coffee shop. "But I wish to tell it before they find me."

Mallory chimed in. "They're small-time criminals, been in and out of prison for theft and drug possession."

The man wearing the stocking cap walked into the coffee shop, quickly glancing at his mobile phone as he entered. The other two men stayed outside.

"One's entered the building," said Jones. "He has a cell phone open."

"That's very interesting," said Thornhill to Golay. "What else can you tell me about your book?" Thornhill locked his eyes on Golay, but he was still able to see the man approaching them trying to conceal the pistol under his large shirt.

Golay looked confused for a moment and then got the hint. "The title would be *Trust*. What do you think?"

"He's looking at a picture of Golay," said Mallory rapidly. "You've all been compromised!"

"Permission to open fire on the hostiles outside," requested Jones.

The man slowly passed their table, first looking at Thornhill and then Golay. He slowed down as he stepped out of Thornhill's view. Thornhill knew the man had found his target.

"Go for it," said Thornhill. And Jones opened fire. A bullet ripped through the black man, entering through the back of his spine and exiting a couple of inches above his belly button. He fell to the ground, dead. Thornhill immediately pulled out his handgun with his right hand and spun around to hit the man behind him, catching him right on the jaw with the butt of his gun. There was the snap of a jaw breaking. The man in the stocking cap fell to the floor, unconscious and bleeding. The third man ran.

"Take him alive!" Thornhill told Jones as he grabbed Golay by the arm and ran out of the Rusland. Golay barely had time to grab his bag from under his chair. A shot came from Jones's position, hitting the fleeing man in the back of the lower leg, tearing out a quarter of his calf. Thornhill aimed his pistol down the street. He could see the third man trying to crawl away, blood gushing from his wound.

"Bring the car around," Thornhill ordered Jones.

"On it," replied Jones.

Pistol ready and with Golay behind him, Thornhill ran up to the third man. He grabbed the man's head and shoved it against the concrete sidewalk. In Dutch, Thornhill asked in a stern, quiet voice, "Who sent you?"

"Go to hell, you bastard!" the man responded through tears of pain as snot ran out of his nose.

Thornhill shoved the man's face into the sidewalk and pressed his foot on the open wound, pushing on the bone. The man let out a muffled scream. Thornhill stopped when the man started answering his question.

"Aldert Fredrick! Aldert Fredrick!"

"Why?"

"He wanted the old man dead! But I don't know why! He didn't tell us anything! Please stop!" Before the thug got a chance to grovel for his life, Thornhill hit him on the back of the head and knocked him unconscious. Thornhill took the man's cell phone out of his pants pocket and searched it for Aldert Fredrick's number. He found it just as Jones arrived with the car. Thornhill returned the phone and pushed Golay into the backseat. They heard the faint sound of police sirens behind them. Jones dodged through streets and alleyways to shake off any pursuers. There were none.

"Mallory," said Thornhill, "I need everything you got on an Aldert Fredrick with this number." He spouted out the number from memory.

"On it," responded Mallory from the car's stereo.

"Also, I need you to track those cell phones and the police coms."

While checking for traffic, Jones stole a glance over his shoulder at Thornhill. "They aren't dead?" Thornhill could hear the frustration in Jones's voice.

"They're both unconscious."

"But they saw you! We're compromised." Jones started to speed up.

"They won't remember. They were looking for Golay, not me. The one inside just glanced at me, and the other one was facing the road." Thornhill was raising his voice to match Jones's.

"You talked to him. He could identify your voice."

"No, he won't! We are not compromised!"

"How do you know?" yelled Jones. "No one knows till it's too late!" He lowered his voice as he slowed the car down and got off the highway. "We must maintain security. No matter the cost."

They sat in silence for a minute as Jones drove the long way back toward their hotel. Mallory's soft voice came over the stereo. "Cross check done. Do you want it now?"

"Yes, please," answered Thornhill in a tired voice. He took out the tablet from the pouch on the back of the driver's seat and looked over what Mallory had found.

"Aldert Fredrick is a pimp," said Mallory.

Thornhill raised an eyebrow as pictures of Aldert Fredrick appeared on his tablet.

"Didn't expect that," said Jones. He sounded calm now.

"He's not just a pimp, though. He's one of the biggest pimps around. He has recently expanded his business to high-class call girls, but his main source of income is street-level girls. It's estimated he has more than one hundred girls working for him on the streets of Amsterdam."

"Seems like he's the biggest of them all, literally," said Thornhill as he examined the pictures on his tablet. Fredrick weighed around three hundred pounds and stood about five foot three. His black hair came down to his shoulders in a ponytail, and a thick goatee almost covered his double chin. "Have you ever seen this man?" Thornhill asked Golay.

Golay shook his head as his hands trembled.

"Did you recognize any of the men who attacked us?"

"No, sorry," Golay said quietly. Thornhill sighed and rubbed his eyes while Jones silently continued to drive around Amsterdam. Mallory intervened.

"The three men received Golay's picture via text. It was taken in a public place. It came with a bounty of three thousand euros for him dead and gave several possible locations for him, including the coffee shop. Here's the list." Mallory sent a list of addresses and pictures of Golay in places ranging from restaurants and museums to parks and bridges.

Thornhill showed the list to Golay and asked, "Did you visit these places regularly? That is, the last time you were in Amsterdam?"

Golay's eyes raced over all the pictures. He slowly nodded, saying nothing. Thornhill saw fear in his eyes.

Thornhill rubbed his face and asked, "Did you leave any vital intel at your hotel?"

Golay tightened his grip on his brown leather bag. "No."

"Good, because you are staying with us till we figure out what to do next, be it abort the mission"—Thornhill looked toward Jones in the rearview mirror—"or continue and find out why this pimp wants you dead."

"The pimp doesn't want me dead," said Golay. "He doesn't care what I am. He's just like the men he sent: a tool, a pawn."

Mallory said, "Sorry to interrupt again, but the police coms are reporting three deaths at the coffee shop. A gang shootout, they are calling it. The descriptions match the three hostiles."

Jones let out a sigh of relief. This puzzled Thornhill, and he felt a pang of guilt. "I guess I hit them harder than I thought," he whispered to himself. Pushing the guilt aside, he proceeded to detail the next step they should take. "All right, Mallory, where can I find this pimp?"

"In the red-light district near De Pijp. Sending you the address now."

"Good. Jones, drop me off here, and then drop by our hotel and check us out. Check into the Blue Tower Hotel we passed on our way from the airport, and when I get back"—Thornhill looked at Golay as the car slowed to a stop at the side of the street—"it's story time."

CHAPTER 6

A CIGAR AND A CIGARETTE

The cab let Thornhill out a few blocks from the red-light district. A tourist would have thought it was like any other collection of apartments with a couple of restaurants and convenience stores dotted throughout, but Thornhill knew better. He saw the prostitutes. Not many were out at this time. They usually waited until dark before they opened their windows for their clients, who varied from rich family men to poor college boys living from paycheck to paycheck. Though the clients varied, the purpose never did.

Thornhill walked to a small café and bought a ham-and-Swiss sandwich with a honey sauce, green apple slices, and butter lettuce, all on a French loaf, served with a side of chips and a bottle of natural water. Thornhill hadn't been sitting outside long when he met the eyes of a girl in her twenties on the other side of the street. She wore four-inch high heels, a denim skirt that barely covered her behind, and a hot-pink

S W ELLENWOOD

tank top revealing her midriff, with a black push-up bra underneath. Her face was slathered in makeup. As the girl crossed the street, Thornhill laid a fifty-euro bill on the end of the table.

She sat down across from him, slowly took the fifty, and said, "You look like a man that needs to let loose," trying to sound sensuous. She brushed a foot against his leg.

Thornhill was unmoved by her attempts to arouse him. He looked her over from head to toe, making it obvious. "A little too old for my taste," he remarked. He took out a hundred-euro bill. "But you could get me what I want. Tell me, are you one of Aldert Fredrick's girls?"

She shifted away from him, taken aback that he knew the name of her pimp. "Yes." Her sexy tone had been replaced by one of caution and fear.

"Good. Go tell him I've heard of his talents. I'd like to have a good time tonight, and I'm willing to pay quite well. Can you do that?" Thornhill handed her the bill, and she slowly took it.

"Of course, but he will want me to come back with a ball-park estimate of what you're willing to spend. He doesn't like to be bothered by customers unless they have the money."

Thornhill could tell she was frightened. "About four thousand euros per girl," he said.

Her eyes widened.

"Tell him this is my last evening here, and I would like to leave with a good feeling. However, I don't have forever. I have a meeting later this afternoon. If he wants my business, he will have to meet me here within an hour. What are you waiting for? I don't think he would treat someone well who caused him to miss out on fifteen thousand euros. Go!" Thornhill shooed her off.

She quickly walked away, almost running, to the other side of the street, where she went a block south to a brick building with a yellow door. Thornhill took out his phone and zoomed in on her. She didn't use the doorbell but knocked twice, paused, and then knocked three times quickly. The door opened. Thornhill made note of the knocks and the lack of a verbal exchange for future reference.

It was about twenty minutes later, after he had finished his sandwich and chips, when Mallory called him over his earpiece.

"Fredrick just called his insider at the police department, asking about a man that fits your description."

"Really?" said Thornhill as he lit a cigar he had brought with him from America. "With prostitution legal in the Netherlands? Wonder what he's hiding."

"His insiders told him they had no undercover cops on him for the time being. Looks like he's going to bite. Are you smoking?" asked Mallory in a concerned voice.

Thornhill smiled. "Maybe."

Mallory huffed.

"Come on," said Thornhill. "I'm in Amsterdam, blending in."

"You're going to blend into a coffin if you keep it up," said Mallory.

Thornhill chuckled. "I'll make sure I won't smell like smoke when I get back. Got to go. Reeling him in now."

The yellow door opened, and Aldert Fredrick stepped out. He was taller than Thornhill had expected but was still as big as ever. One hand held a phone to his ear, and he had a pack of cigarettes in the other hand.

"Be safe," said Mallory.

Fredrick hung up, adjusted his jeans, and smoothed out the wrinkles in his tropical shirt. He ran his fingers through his greasy black hair, which hung in a ponytail. After he crossed the street, he sat down across from Thornhill, breathing heavily. Thornhill spoke as Fredrick caught his breath.

"Aldert Fredrick?" Thornhill reached out his hand to shake the pimp's. The man's grip was firm but had no power behind it.

"I am. And you are?" asked Fredrick. His voice hardly had a Dutch accent to it, which placed him as a longtime resident of the Netherlands, but not a native. His English was too good for that.

"Mr. Smith," responded Thornhill.

"Mr. Smith, nice to meet you. So, one of my girls said you would like to have a good time tonight?"

"Not tonight." Fredrick frowned at the prospect that he'd been lied to. "Tomorrow will be the night. I just wanted to make sure I got a chance to talk to you."

Fredrick sighed in relief. "Glad to hear. So what do you want? For four thousand euros, the options are almost endless."

"Oh, the four thousand is just a deposit. I plan to pay double afterward." Fredrick stared wide-eyed at him, speechless. Thornhill took a puff of his cigar.

Without breaking his stare, Fredrick took out a cigarette and lit it. "What's the catch?" he asked, taking a drag of his cigarette.

Thornhill tapped ash from his cigar onto the ground. "I want three girls, English speaking, good busts but not too big, shorter than me, pretty faces, no tattoos. Also, I want a nice place too—a roomy hotel room."

"And?"

"One should be a redhead, another a brunette, and the last a blonde."

"And?"

"They should be young."

"There it is. How young? Nineteen? Eighteen?" Fredrick tapped ashes off his cigarette.

"Between fourteen and sixteen, and virgins. Can you do that?"

Fredrick didn't break eye contact, though Thornhill could see the gears in his mind turning. Fredrick nodded slowly and said, "I can do that."

"Good. Listen, I have to go to a meeting at the moment, but let's have dinner tonight around eight, and you can bring some options, how about that?"

"That sounds perfect. How about you come to my restaurant as my honored guest? Do you like sushi?"

"I love it."

"Wonderful. Here is the address, and I'll start looking for the girls right away." Fredrick handed him a business card for his Japanese steakhouse. They both stood as Fredrick hailed a cab for Thornhill.

"Excellent," said Thornhill. "I have high hopes for to-morrow night, and if it goes as well as I hope, I may recommend you to my friends with similar tastes and wallets as me."

"It will be the greatest night of your life. I will find the purest and most beautiful young girls you will ever lay eyes and lips on." A taxi stopped in front of them, and Fredrick opened the door for Thornhill.

"I certainly hope so. See you tonight." Thornhill stepped inside the taxicab, and Fredrick closed the door behind him. As the taxi drove off, Thornhill glanced back at Fredrick. He stood there for a moment and then skipped like a little boy all the way to the building with the yellow door. Thornhill turned back around. Yes, he had made Aldert Fredrick a happy man…for the present.

CHAPTER 7

STUFFED BEARS

Thornhill knocked three times on the door of room 323 at the Blue Tower Hotel. Jones opened the door.

"Everything go well?" he asked as Thornhill walked into one of the only hotel rooms in Amsterdam that had three beds in it.

Thornhill laid his coat on the middle bed, followed by his entire body. "It went well. I feel like taking a disinfecting shower, though, after talking to that scumbag. Where's Golay?"

"Bathroom. Learn anything?" asked Jones as he sat down in the wooden chair near the window.

Thornhill turned over on to his back and stared at the white ceiling. Then he looked at Jones and the dark-red curtains behind him covering the window from prying eyes. "No, but I did set up a meeting with him tonight at eight for dinner and to talk about some girls. During dinner, I will try to see if he knows Golay at all. If I don't get good enough intel from him, one of us will have to infiltrate his home, either tonight or tomorrow. Maybe tomorrow. Today has been rough."

Jones laughed. He was cleaning his rifle.

"Did you have any trouble getting the room?" asked Thornhill.

"No," said Jones. "Mallory set it up well. By the time we walked in and gave our aliases, we already had a reservation, made a month ago, or so it appeared. No one followed us, either."

"Good to hear." Thornhill closed his eyes for a little rest before Golay got out of the bathroom. "Thanks for covering Golay and me back there."

Jones shrugged. "Just doing my job. I'm...I'm sorry about earlier...questioning you. I've just..." He stopped cleaning his rifle and stared at the floor. "I've just seen what happens when people let the enemy slip away because of something inside of them. It comes back to bite them."

Thornhill sat up and looked at the burnt-orange carpet before turning his gaze to Jones. "I understand. I won't let it happen again, because you're right. We must maintain security."

Jones lifted his eyes to meet Thornhill's.

Thornhill added, "No matter the cost."

"No matter the cost," replied Jones.

Golay exited the bathroom, wiping his hands with a towel.

"Good. Now, let's get started." Thornhill sat up with his back against the bed's headboard. Golay pulled up a chair near the end of the bed farthest from Jones, who was still cleaning his gun. "To begin, what's in the bag?" asked Thornhill.

Golay took his brown bag from under the desk behind him and placed it on his lap. "You didn't go through it yet?" he asked sarcastically.

"I didn't have enough time. Do you want me to go through it now?" replied Jones in a snarky tone.

Golay held the bag a tad tighter, like a child with a stuffed bear. "No need. I'll tell you. It's evidence. Enough evidence to prove their existence, but not enough to convict them, because if it was, I would be publishing it everywhere I went, going door to door if I had to."

"Existence of what?" asked Thornhill. "What is it proving?"

"Let me tell you my story first. Then I will let you be the judge of the evidence I have. First, what do you know about me?"

"Basics. You lived in America when you were a child and then moved back to Switzerland with your mother after your father died. Worked at a bank under the order of an NSA anticommunist division looking for communist money. A couple of years later, it closed down, and you disappeared. Did I miss anything?"

"Spot on for all the official stuff, I would say."

"My handler can make a mean report. But reports are for a broad view. I want to zoom in and see what you saw, and see your 'evidence' before we make any judgment calls. So, your story?"

"Yes, my story. Where to begin?"

"Start with a dark and stormy night. That is such a unique start to a story," said Thornhill. Jones gave a small chuckle.

"To be honest, I can't really remember what the weather was like that night. I was a little too preoccupied with trying not to drown," said Golay.

CHAPTER 8

AN OLD MAN'S STORY

"Let me give you some backstory first. When my mother and I were about to move back to Switzerland, she had some money trouble. Even selling the family business wasn't enough to get us over there, and that's not even considering where we were going to live. I think she planned on us living with my grandmother. If that had happened, I would have swum back to America in a heartbeat. Don't get me wrong. I loved my grandmother—may she rest in peace—but I could only stand her in small amounts, like a beer, except you skip the drunk stage and go straight to the hangover.

"Where was I? Moving, right. So, we had money trouble for getting over to Switzerland. I was, at the time, finishing up my degree in accounting and working full time as a janitor at the NSA headquarters. How? I had met a student at the university whose father was high up in the NSA food chain. Our families became great friends, and he helped me land the janitor job. The father heard about how my mother and I were trying to get back to Switzerland. He called me into his office about a year before we left. I remember that day vividly. The smoky room, my file on his glass desk, and a giant cigar hanging out of his small mouth.

"'Golay, glad you could make it. Please have a seat,' he said.

"I thanked him and sat down. He continued, 'You know what makes America great?'

"Fear grew inside of me. Not a fear of something I had done, but of what was going to happen to me. I answered, 'Freedom?'

"'Yes, freedom. The freedom to live as we please, to pursue our dreams. That's the American dream right there.' He took a long puff of his cigar and said, 'I hear you and your mother are moving back to Switzerland?'

"My heart leaped to my throat. 'Yes, most of our family still lives there, and the past couple of years have been hard on her since Dad passed,' I said.

"He nodded in agreement. 'Understandable. It is a lot easier to get past such a hardship with family members close by. It will be a shame to see you go. Your supervisor always gave you high praise for your work and loyalty.'

"'It's been a great time, working here,' I said. 'My supervisor has been very helpful working with my hours as a student.'

"'I admire that.' He pointed his bony finger at me. 'It takes a lot to go through school and work at the same time.

Not that many people have the privilege of being a full-time student, and usually it's the undeserving brats who get that blessing. When will you two be leaving?' he asked.

"'When we have enough money to travel over there and buy a house,' I told him. 'A couple of years, at least.'

"He nodded and said, 'You're a smart young man, Golay. Hard worker, loyal, patriotic. Since you are a Swiss citizen with an accounting degree from the United States, it shouldn't be too hard for you to get a job. Am I right?'

"'I certainly hope so, sir.'

"'Where will you work?'

"'Wherever will hire me, sir.'

"'Would you consider working at a bank?'

"'Yes, sir.'

"'Before I continue, let me ask you one more question. What are your thoughts about communism?'

"'I think it is the worst form of government ever. Well, second worst. A dictatorship is a little worse in my eyes. Though the two aren't much different, are they, sir?'

"He ignored my question and asked, 'And what would you do to stop it from spreading?'

"At this point, I was stuck between two completely different feelings. Part of me was still fearful of what he wanted me to do. I was scared he was going to send me over to Switzerland to kill someone and then take the fall for it. Yet I was still curious. I remember I took a moment to choose my words carefully, hoping to satisfy my curiosity and not be turned into a scapegoat. I was sweating like a fountain under my janitor outfit. My mouth had dried up, but I answered his question. 'I would do whatever it took if it didn't involve hurting anyone.'

"He smiled and said, 'That's what I wanted to hear.'

"Over the next year, I was trained in the basics: code breaking, forging signatures, removing fingerprints, the Russian language, and some weapons training in case the worst happened, which it did. My mother never knew about it, and I'm glad she didn't. I don't think she would've seen the positive side of it. She didn't understand the world terribly well. She was a very black-and-white lady, a good side and bad side kind of person, you know. She didn't see the world the way it was or where it was going, moving to being more gray all around, bad guys hidden among good guys and vice versa.

"But being just a janitor, I saw it. I noticed the tension. Another janitor I worked with made a joke to a fellow co-worker about our government, or a positive comment about communism—I can't remember—and the next day, he was being questioned. A week later, he was fired. I mean, it could have been worse for him and his family, but still, I won't forget the look on his face when he was gathering his things. I knew him. He was a patriotic man. He loved America. He fought in World War II. He was at Normandy. And here the country he fought for, suffered for, the country he killed for, fired him...

"What? Oh, sorry. Back to the story. So, when I got all my training done, the NSA paid for the plane ride and a house for us to live in over in Switzerland. It was a nice little house. It was about thirty minutes outside of Zurich in the middle of nowhere, but it was a beautiful house that cost us nothing. I will never forget that.

"As my mother got us settled in, I went to every major bank that dealt with international transactions looking for a job, and I got nowhere. A month's worth of job searching, and I was still at square one. So I started applying for any position in any bank, not just accounting. Went on doing that for another month, and still nothing. With my bank account dwindling and my mother finding out she had leukemia, it was a hard time. I remember I had just finished another day of trying to make connections that led nowhere and walked into the kitchen to see my mother staring at the sink. I could tell she'd been crying—her eyes were red and puffy. What a clever spy I was! I asked her what was wrong, and she told me.

"It's hard to explain the feeling of being a total failure at life. I felt like I had failed my country, my ideals, my mother. I felt like crawling into a hole to hide from my shame, where no one could hear me as I screamed at myself like a madman. It was a feeling of failure that only some people feel, once in their lifetime, where you either come out the other side a stronger man or you let it eat you alive. I remember sitting on my bed that night after my mother had cried herself to sleep. I sat with the pistol the NSA had given me in my hands. It felt heavier than before. I would be lying if I told you I didn't entertain the idea of killing myself. I then had a moment of...

"Sorry, I'm getting sidetracked again. In short, we got through that tough time, though it wasn't easy. A month later, I got the chance I was looking for. I was in the pharmacy, getting my mother her pills and talking to the pharmacist. By this time, my mother and I had already been in there enough to be on a first-name basis with the pharmacist. Well, while we were talking, he mentioned his son. I think he was about to go to college, and he needed to quit his job working as a janitor for this small company that did the janitorial work for many businesses around Zurich, including several of the major banks. So I asked him where I could apply, and he told me. The next day, I went down to their office with no more than a house, a sick mother, and three francs to my name. I walked into the front room, and I handed the girl sitting behind the desk my résumé. She looked at it and then looked up at me and asked, 'Are you Matt's dad's friend?'

"'Um, yes?' I replied uncertainly.

"'Well, you're a fast one.' She stood up, walked over to a small closet, took out two blue janitor uniforms and a single hat, and gave them to me. 'The janitors meet here at eight in the evening every day and work till four in the morning, or not that late if you all are having a good night.'

"'So, I got the job?' I asked.

"'I wouldn't be handing you these if you didn't,' she said.

"I sat down in the chair behind me and cried. After months of hardship and worry, I had found a job. It took the girl by surprise as she stood there with my new uniforms. I got up, wiped my tears, thanked her for everything, took the uniforms from her hands, and went home, with a detour to the pharmacy to thank the pharmacist.

"The first couple of months, we were doing well. Being a janitor didn't pay nearly as well as an accountant, but it was a livable income. I didn't try to gather any intel at first. I just spent my time learning my job and keeping my eyes open for opportunities for the future. It was routine kind of work, which made my spying easier later.

"It wasn't until my fourth month on the job that I decided to make a move. Another janitor who helped me with one of the floors of a bank we cleaned on Friday was sick. My boss offered to call in someone to help me, but I told him I could handle it. My heart was racing at the time, seeing as I was at the doorstep of what I'd been sent over for. I rode with the rest of the janitors to the bank. No, I don't recall the bank's name. It did, however, take care of a lot of foreign transactions. I cleaned my floor as fast as I could, taking care only of places I knew people would notice and leaving the rest. Once I was done, I put on my winter gloves and looked around for anything useful, searching in the foreign transaction papers. Sadly, I found nothing of interest, so I joined up with the rest of the janitors and left.

"As the days continued, I found ways to look for information while cleaning, sneaking a look here and there while my fellow janitor cleaned on the other side of the floor or in the bathroom. As time passed, it became easier to spy. I gathered what information I could, though I found nothing related even remotely to the communist cause. I continued to do this for a couple of years, getting nowhere in finding communist international funding. I did, however, start finding—how do I put it?—fishy transactions. That was partly because of where I found them: only in the bank president's office.

"What were they? Oh, I have some pictures of them, so you can see. Here…as you can see, they were large and strange amounts of money. I usually saw rounded numbers, but these never had a zero in them. They were never the same amount and were always cash withdrawals straight from the bank. The receiver was never listed. I sent what I learned to the NSA to see if it was related to the communists in any way, but it wasn't. They said it didn't follow their codes: it was too small, or something like that. They said it could have been some bank backdoor dealing or something. They showed no interest in it at first, so I stopped reporting about it until I checked the other banks. I discovered that two others had the same thing happening, and the documentation was found in the same place: the bank president's office. They had the same amount of money cashed out on the same day. I reported that back and heard nothing from the NSA for three weeks.

"Then I got the letter saying that my division was closed down. No signs, no warning, nothing. Just one letter, and it was all over. I tried to call my handler, but the line was already disconnected.

"Then my mother died.

"I know that may seem irrelevant, but that and the letter were the reasons for my long vacation across Europe. I visited London, Paris, Florence, and ended the trip by visiting Amsterdam, where I found it. What was it? The connection. The whole trip was basically a mourning time for me. It was only by sheer chance that one day, while wandering about Amsterdam, I found the coffee shop we met at, the Rusland. That's where I met her. Joy. I sat down and ordered the same drink you got for me, an espresso, and as I sat there contemplating life, I saw a young, beautiful lady. She sat where you sat, reading the same book you read, and eating the same sandwich as you did. Joy had long, bright-red hair. She would be called fat by the standards of today, but she wasn't. She was beautiful. Her face was kind, and—

"Pardon? Oh, yes. Sorry. Well, she caught me looking at her, and after a little bit of across-the-room flirting, I went over to her table and struck up a conversation. In the end, we decided to meet up for dinner at an Italian place somewhere down the road. The night was amazing. I had great food and beautiful company. We talked for so long that the restaurant employees were waiting for us to leave before they could close. We talked about everything: life, hobbies, dreams, family, loss. After dinner, we went back to her place for coffee and to continue our conversation. I think it was four in the morning before I left. I know that I had only known her for a day, but I knew Joy was different. We continued to see each other a lot over the next couple of days. She showed me around Amsterdam, the grand things all the tourists go to see, but also the hidden beauties of the city the tourists could never find, even with all their maps and tour guides. It may have been the death of my mother that caused me to fall in love with her in such a short time. I don't know.

"Well, on my last night in Amsterdam, Joy took me to this little family-owned restaurant a couple of blocks from the beach. I can't even remember what they served us, because I was so infatuated with her beauty. She wore an orange sleeveless dress with a black neckline. It was a slim dress that came down to about midthigh, and she wore these black, almost skintight boots that came a little above her knees. I know it sounds absurd, but that was the hottest thing in fashion those days. And boy, did she look gorgeous. Her fingernails even matched her dress. After dinner, we went for a walk on the beach. It was a beautiful night: full moon, the sound of the sea caressing the shore. We strolled for a bit in silence before walking under a pier. That's when I stopped her. The moonlight shone between the boards on to her eyes, like a bandit's mask. And right then and there, I confessed my love to her and told her how she had changed my world and—

"Yes? Oh, well…as this was happening, a car drove onto the pier. It parked at the far end and just sat there. About ten minutes passed, and then a large truck with a car behind it drove onto the pier. I checked my watch, and it was one in the morning, so of course we both grew curious. We quietly waded into the sea to get within earshot of the conversation. To my surprise, they were speaking Russian. With my recent employment, this worried me, and I told her to stay back as I took some of my clothes off and quietly swam down to the end of the pier. The current was strong as I neared the pier's end. I grabbed hold of one of the wooden pillars and climbed up closer to hear them better. There was a deep Russian voice, a perfect stereotype of Russian high authority. The other voice was a little higher, with an accent that I couldn't put my finger on. He also referred to himself as a group. The higher voice spoke of a Czechoslovakian revolt that was going to take place, with all the information on it in a file. The deeper voice informed him that the money was in the truck. I heard footsteps go toward the truck. The truck doors opened and then closed. I heard a pair of keys exchange hands, and someone had started to walk away, when I heard Joy scream.

"They had found her and dragged her on top of the pier. The deeper voice started yelling at Joy, asking questions: if she was alone and why she was here. She thought of a good lie to tell, but it didn't matter. I saw two men with flashlights and rifles come down to the beach and start searching under the pier. I climbed down and swam to the far end of the pier, slowly freezing and holding on as tight as I could behind one of the pillars. They didn't search long. It was hard to hear what they said because of the waves hitting the beach and crushing me against the wooden pillar. I then heard footsteps come up to the edge of the pier right above me. The higher voice demanded that I give myself up or...or else. Joy kept yelling, trying to convince them she was the only one there. I heard a loud crack and her scream as the man shouted again, saying it was my last chance. I said nothing, hanging on to the wood pillar as tight as I could. My fingers grew numb with every passing second. Only the sound of the waves and her weeping filled the air.

"The voice then said, 'I guess you were right.' A gunshot rang out, and she fell into the water right in front of me, dead, her blood flowing out from her head toward me, surrounding me, splashing against me with the waves. I had killed her. Joy's blood was on my hands because of my cowardice, my selfishness. As they drove off, her floating hair started wrapping around me. I made a vow to avenge her on this enemy, this enemy with no name."

CHAPTER 9

NO CRUMWELL

"I searched for years after that night, but came up with very little, if anything at all. When the Czechoslovakian revolt started and ended within the same week, I knew that this enemy was bigger than I thought. So I moved about, working at banks around Europe with different aliases, looking at everything I could get my hands on for over fifty years." Golay placed the bag on the floor. "This is the work of that fifty years."

Thornhill was puzzled. He checked the time. He hadn't known Golay would be this long in telling his story. Thornhill had a half hour to get to his meeting with the pimp. He rose from the bed and went to the bathroom to change his outfit as he asked Golay some questions.

"So, the main reason for this meeting was to inform us about this hidden group and to hand us the information you have collected on them, correct?"

"Yes."

"Yet you still don't know their name?"

"No, but this will prove their existence!"

"Prove their existence and convict them?"

Golay was quiet for a second. "It's possible."

Thornhill sighed in disappointment and said, "Jones, your thoughts?"

"Looks like a dead end, I would say, if we hadn't run into those goons earlier at the coffee shop. There could be something here."

"I agree," responded Thornhill as he came out of the bathroom, putting on his suit jacket. "You two should look over the stuff Golay brought and see what you can find while I have sushi." Thornhill was a little happy that he at least was going to have sushi that night.

"With a man who sells sex," added Jones.

Thornhill felt nauseated by the idea. He hid his pistol in his slim-fit suit. "At least I get sushi."

Thornhill walked down to the parking garage, got the BMW, and left for the Japanese steakhouse Fredrick owned, on Prins Hendrikkade near the canal. As he drove, he called Mallory and reported Golay's story for her to check out.

"So, Jones is going over what Golay has while I meet up with Fredrick," Thornhill said as he turned onto the highway.

"You don't believe him?" asked Mallory.

"No. His story had a lot of personal details, which I think he used to make it sound authentic. Though the people trying to kill us does show that there is something here. Does any of his story check out?"

"Some of it," said Mallory. "His mother, however, died in a house fire, and there's no company that did the janitorial work for all the major banks. They each hired their own, for security reasons. Also, there's no evidence of him traveling around Europe. Did he tell you the alias he used?"

"No." Thornhill stopped at a stoplight. Watching tourists and natives of Amsterdam crossing the street a couple of cars ahead of him, he wondered about the Russians. "I don't think he trusts me. Did his story about the Russians check out?"

Mallory was silent for a time before saying, "Maybe. A Russian major general, Dmitriy Kirillovsky, traveled from Moscow to Amsterdam. A week after the revolt, he was promoted to colonel general."

"Was there mention of a source?"

"No. Golay did open up a Swiss bank account a month before he left, and he closed it within a week after the pier meeting. However, there are no records of any transactions made with it."

Thornhill pulled over in front of a beauty shop within sight of the restaurant, called Higashi-bi, which is Japanese for East Sun. He could see Fredrick in a triple-large black suit with a light-brown striped tie. He was showing his goons, probably for the tenth time, how to act when Thornhill arrived. One looked annoyed, checking his mobile phone every two seconds, waiting for a text from a girl, Thornhill assumed. The other was pulling at his collar as if he had a noose around his neck, though it was just a ten-euro bow tie.

Thornhill decided to wait until it looked like Fredrick had everything under control before he drove up. He stroked his chin as if he had a beard. He enjoyed growing his beard out during his vacation, though Mallory didn't like it that much.

"So, what we have is an old NSA agent who may have found a Swiss bank laundering money, a Russian general buying secrets, and a dead girlfriend, and the same people may be behind it all," he said to himself out loud. "In any other setting, I would say this is just a wild goose chase, but he knew Crumwell. Yet he didn't mention him at all in his story. And someone is trying to kill him. But why?"

"I don't know," responded Mallory. "I just have a bad feeling about this whole mission."

Thornhill snickered. "The same bad feeling you had on that hike?"

"With the sun setting behind it, that dead tree looked a lot like a bear!" Mallory sounded irritated, but she couldn't keep herself from chuckling as Thornhill laughed out loud.

As the laughing died down, they both sat in silence for a moment. Mallory hung up after saying, "Just be careful."

Thornhill leaned on the steering wheel, contemplating Fredrick, who was checking his cell phone. Thornhill took a deep breath, getting ready to play his part, and asked himself under his breath, "Who's your boss, Fredrick?"

CHAPTER 10

SUSHI AND THE PIMP

Thornhill drove up to Higashi-bi in his rented black BMW. The goon choking on his tie opened the car door for him. For a thug, he held himself well, back straight, unused hand behind his back. The other guy stood by the door, ready to open it at any moment. Thornhill stepped out of the car. Fredrick reached out for a handshake as Thornhill handed his keys to the valet.

"Mr. Smith, I hope you are ready for the best meal of your life." Frederick's hand was quite sweaty, contrary to Thornhill's expectations. He assumed that this was Fredrick's biggest deal yet. (Sadly, it was his second, as Thornhill later found out.)

"I'm prepared to be amazed," replied Thornhill, patting Fredrick on the back.

The doorman opened the door for them with great posture, to Thornhill's surprise. Fredrick and Thornhill were seated immediately, ahead of the tourist family that Thornhill had seen earlier at the airport and a group of well-dressed high-school students, who looked rather upset as Thornhill and Fredrick passed them without having to wait. They were led to the end of the restaurant, passing between the bar and tables full of people, all of the guests dressed in their best attire. Each table had a teppanyaki grill with a chef at it, cooking for and entertaining the diners, creating small trains out of onions, catching eggs in their hats, and making volcanos from oil and a match. The two reached their table at the end of the restaurant, between the bar and the end of a long mural that ran the length of the wall. The mural depicted the Japanese countryside, with jagged mountains, cherry trees in bloom, and waterfalls falling into the abyss below the mountains.

Once they were seated, a young waitress came over and asked for their drink order. Thornhill ordered an arrack, a distilled alcohol from Southeast Asia, commonly made from the fermented sap of coconut flowers or sugarcane. Fredrick ordered a beer. Their drinks came a couple of minutes later, along with a dragon sushi dish, different types of sushi lined up in the shape of a dragon, with various dipping sauces for the wings and fire made of red wasabi. Fredrick then ordered the main course: teriyaki chicken with white rice and grilled vegetables.

"Before we talk business, I have one more thing for you." From his inside coat pocket, Fredrick took an Ashton Heritage Puro Sol cigar, a slim yet rich and flavorful cigar.

Thornhill took it out of its plastic pouch and inhaled deeply. He could smell the hint of coffee and chocolate in the African tobacco.

"That smells lovely. You know how to treat a man right, Fredrick. Have you ever thought of moving up from street hoes to call girls?" Thornhill placed the cigar back in its pouch, saving it for after dinner.

"I have, a little. The street hoes, however, are the bread and butter of my operation. To be honest, you are one of my highest-paying clients to date. Also, how did you hear about me?" Thornhill saw through Fredrick's fake smile and noted the concern in his eyes, like a territorial animal.

"Well, I have had some friends travel through here before for business, and they wanted to relax," Thornhill explained. "They called up the local escort services but were never really satisfied. They would just send a girl, no regard for what my friends did or didn't like, charging unbelievable prices, and you had to do it in your hotel room, and most of the time, they traveled with other coworkers. Very unprofessional, in my opinion."

"Of course."

"However, I had a friend who came through a couple of times and said what he did was call up the window prostitutes or street hoes and meet up with their boss and give him his request for a reasonable price, and it worked quite well. He said his best experience was with you."

"Really? What was his name?"

"Golay, Nils Golay."

Fredrick looked to the left and tilted his head to the right as if trying to remember who that was. "I don't remember that name," he said, finally. "It may have been through one of my lower-level fellows." Fredrick took a sip of his beer as Thornhill observed him and came to the conclusion that he was telling the truth.

"Probably. Well, anyway, he told me of the great experience he had, and I knew I needed a man with that kind of customer-centered mind-set to fulfill my particular tastes, but not a snob like the high-class-escorts men, who would just throw me whatever girl was free that night—if you could call her a girl."

They laughed and started making jokes about the ugly women they had seen in their lives or, in Fredrick's case, had "banged," as he put it. Once the jokes had ceased, to Thornhill's delight, he saw that Fredrick was becoming more comfortable. Thornhill directed the conversation to the business at hand. He planned to find out more about Fredrick after the meeting.

The chef cooked their food. They ate, enjoying it, while Fredrick showed Thornhill pictures of teenage girls with their height, weight, age, and bust size. Thornhill made sure to take his time, making it seem as if he enjoyed talking about which girl had the better breasts. He tried to focus on all of a girl's characteristics: her eyes, smile, hair, even her complexion. But Fredrick always brought it back to two things—boobs and ass. After the meal and twenty pictures of underage girls, Thornhill had picked three of them: a fifteen-year-old redhead, a fifteen-year-old brunette, and a sixteen-year-old blonde. According to Fredrick, they were visiting from Germany and wanted to have a good time, though Thornhill knew that wasn't true.

As dessert came, a mochi ice cream, Thornhill could tell Fredrick was getting a little tipsy. Thornhill took the opportunity to ask him how he'd gotten into this business, hoping Fredrick would let slip a piece of information that could be useful to him, whatever it might be.

Fredrick chuckled. "Well, it's an interesting story." With careful and delicate words of persuasion, Thornhill got Fredrick to tell him his full story.

CHAPTER 11

A PIMP'S TRUTH

Aldert Fredrick had had a normal childhood by all accounts. He was born and raised in America. He watched football, ate pizza, discovered porn, smoked weed, hung out with friends, looked at porn, skipped school, hit on girls, and watched porn, until he was eighteen. He took a trip to Europe with a group of friends, enjoying the sights, the food, and the women, but mostly the women, though he had no luck with any of them. It didn't take long until he started running out of money. But while in Amsterdam planning his return home with his friends, he found he had enough money to stay an extra two nights at the small, sketchy motel and give himself a birthday present.

He lied and told his friends that he had family in Amsterdam and was going to visit them for his birthday the next day. He saw his friends all off at the airport. After they left, he bought a ticket for a flight back to America the next day. He then went back to his motel, packed up for tomorrow, and went and got dinner at a small café by himself. He was hardly hungry. He'd had butter-flies in his stomach ever since his decision. He hailed a taxi and went to the red-light district of Amsterdam.

Aldert got out of the cab near the edge of the district. He walked down the street, his heart beating faster, his hands sweating, his mouth drying up. After about a five-minute walk, he reached the heart of the red-light district. He looked up at the old buildings in amazement. Women filled a few of the windows, wearing bras and bikinis, teasing the prod-uct to the customers. Not that many people were out on the street. A couple of local college students walked down it, de-ciding which woman would be perfect for a gang bang. A married man took off his wedding ring and placed it in his wallet as he took out his money to pay for the night, giving it to a tall, black-haired man standing in front of one of the doors. An elderly man stood inside a phone booth, looking up at the buildings with his hands in his pants.

It took a little longer then Aldert expected to pick the girl he wanted. The range of women was quite wide, from flat-chested white chicks to busty Asian girls. Aldert wanted to have sex with them all. However, his wallet said no. It wasn't until a new prod-uct came on the line did he make his decision. On the top floor, a light came on, and a black girl with a cigarette stepped into the light. Her long hair was almost as white as snow. She wore a red C cup bra, Aldert's favorite size. He walked up to the door of the house. No man stood there, so he knocked. A young, skin-ny man wearing a white tank top opened the door. He looked around twenty-five, with a goatee and pierced ears and a joint between his lips. The dude asked Aldert which girl he wanted and for how long—an hour or all night? Aldert described the girl and asked about prices. He paid one hundred dollars to have sex with the blond black girl all night.

Aldert awoke late the next morning, relishing the experience among the stained, black bedsheets. The girl showered in the bathroom, washing away the night. He heard a knock on the door, and a small man came in and told him it was time to go. Aldert got up and was putting on his pants when the girl came out of the bathroom, a dirty towel wrapped round her body. Aldert looked at her, her wet hair coming down to the top of her backside. Her green eyes were puffy from the tears she'd shed in the shower, but Aldert didn't notice. He just stared at her body and asked for one for the road. She sighed and uncovered herself to fill his bottomless pit of lust. As Aldert left, he saw, across the hallway, a poorly dressed older fellow giving a duffel bag to a well-dressed younger man. As the younger man turned around, Aldert saw that he was missing half of one eyebrow.

Thornhill's phone rang.

"I'm so sorry." Thornhill took out his cell phone. He didn't recognize the number. He answered with caution, giving a cheerful hello.

"Thornhill! It's Golay. Jones has been shot! The hotel has been compromised. Meet me at the Rederij Lovers boat tour in thirty minutes."

CHAPTER 12

GLASS FORTRESS

Mallory paced through Glass's underground fortress in Detroit, a hidden contribution to the city's recent rebirth, passing through an open two-story area with a conference table on one side and a rock wall on the other. Seated at the table, CIA, NSA, and FBI operatives, support staff, and handlers worked on the situation in the Middle East. Mallory caught a glimpse of one of them reading about the disappearance of a cargo ship in Southeast Asia. At the end of the floor space, occupying one corner was Crumwell's office, elevated a story above the floor, giving the director of Glass an overview of the battleground. Mallory ascended the tight spiral staircase to his glass-encased office.

"Yes, General...Your faith in this branch will not be in vain...Understood. You will be the first to know...Of course. Good-bye." Crumwell hung up the phone and assessed Mallory as she walked in. She tilted her head to the window, her fingers drumming on the tablet she clutched tightly to her chest. Crumwell made a lowering gesture with his hand, as if he were a magician delevitating his assistant. Steel walls emerged from the ceiling and encased them in privacy. Mallory sat down across from Crumwell and gave him the bad news.

"Jones got shot. Golay is on the run." Her voice was quick but calm. Her fingers still drummed on the tablet.

"How long ago was this?"

"Fifteen minutes ago."

"What's Jones's condition?"

"Unknown."

"Where's Thornhill?"

"Leaving his meeting with Fredrick to meet up with Golay."

"Where?"

"He didn't tell me. His precise words were, 'Jones was shot. Golay is on the run. Will call back.' He had about a good two hours with Fredrick, so I assume he got some info from him."

Crumwell gave a heavy sigh, leaning back in his chair and looking at the silver ceiling. Mallory noticed his right hand trembling.

"Did Thornhill report his verdict on Golay before the meeting?" Crumwell asked, taking out his pipe from the top drawer of his desk.

"Yes, and he didn't trust him."

"Why not?" Crumwell stuffed tobacco into his pipe.

"Golay's story didn't match the facts."

"Was Jones there?"

Mallory thought the question odd, but she answered it all the same. "To my knowledge, he was."

Crumwell lit his pipe, inhaled the smoke, and then exhaled it in a long, slow breath. The smoke rose slowly to the ceiling and spread above them until it was nothing but a sweet smell. Mallory held her breath. She didn't approve of her boss's smoking habit, but she never said anything. Crumwell gripped his pipe in his teeth and, with shaky hands, picked up his secure cell phone and texted Thornhill a one-word message. He leaned back and took another puff.

"How do you think they were compromised?" asked Crumwell.

"I don't know, sir. I think once Thornhill gets back with what he learned from Fredrick, we will have a better idea of what's going on and start connecting some dots." Mallory purposefully avoided what she feared was the truth.

"But do you really think a pimp would have a motive against an old retired NSA agent who hasn't been to Amsterdam in years?"

Mallory gulped. "Maybe? You never know. Golay could be lying about something that could connect both of them, or—"

Crumwell interrupted her. "According to your report, Fredrick arrived in Amsterdam ten years after Golay left, and Golay hasn't been back until now. So what happened, Mallory? What do you fear happened?"

Mallory leaned forward to whisper, "There's a mole inside Glass feeding the pimp, or more likely whoever the pimp is working for, information."

Crumwell nodded and took another puff from his pipe. "Do you believe that the Silence channels are flawed?"

"Possibly. What other options are there?" Mallory hoped he wouldn't accuse her, or worse, Thornhill, of being the mole.

Crumwell watched the smoke rising from his pipe. "Start searching the Amsterdam hospitals for Jones, and bring me an emergency backpack and a suitcase."

CHAPTER 13

THE LOVE BOAT

Thornhill sat beside Golay in the stern of the Rederij Lovers boat with his pistol pressed right against Golay's ribs as Golay clutched his brown bag. The boat slowly started down the canal for its evening ride, popular among young tourist couples. There weren't that many couples on this trip, since this was the last tour of the night. The captain said a few words, advising people to stay seated and keep their arms and legs inside the boat at all times, adding that they didn't have to keep them to themselves. The couples giggled. Thornhill chuckled with them, but Golay did not. The captain started the romantic music as he pulled out from the dock and into the canal. Once they'd been out on the canal for a couple of minutes, Thornhill spoke.

"Tell me the truth."

"I did," Golay whispered. "I put myself on the line, and this is how you repay me? At gunpoint?"

Thornhill saw through the lie. "This mission didn't begin well, and I don't plan on it ending well," he said, admiring the scenery discreetly while aiming the barrel of his pistol upward, toward Golay's heart.

Golay breathed out slowly, looking toward the opposite side of the canal.

Thornhill continued. "I know that this mission was off the books, and yet some lowlife pimp is sending thugs to—"

"Do you trust Jones?" Golay's voice quivered as he asked the question.

"How can I trust *you*? You lied to us about your background, about almost everything."

"What did my letter say?" Frustration grew in Golay's voice. "I sent that letter to Crumwell in faith that he himself or another would come in under the radar and receive the information I had and use it against them! But he didn't! He didn't come."

Golay lowered his head, and Thornhill saw a small tear fall from Golay's eye. A tear from a lost old man or a tear from a crocodile, Thornhill couldn't decide. Thornhill thought about Jones, how he knew him, mostly in passing. He had never really talked with Jones before this mission. He'd trained with him some. However, Thornhill was in a separate training program. (His colleagues referred to him as the alpha tester, since he was the only trainee in that program.) Jones had seemed quite relieved when they'd found out that all the thugs from the coffee shop were dead. Were they loose ends? And if they were, whose loose ends were they? Thornhill entertained the idea of a mole in Glass…possibly named Jones. These ideas all quickly drifted from his mind when he thought about Golay's earlier question. "What do you mean, do I trust Jones? What happened at the hotel? Why did you leave him?" A shiver went up Thornhill's spine.

"Jones got shot."

"Who shot him?"

Golay closed his eyes and told what Thornhill thought was the truth for the first time. "I did."

Thornhill applied pressure on the trigger of his gun, pausing only because his cell phone vibrated in his pocket. He released his finger from the trigger and took out his phone to read the message Crumwell had sent. Thornhill put his gun away, and Golay released a sigh of relief.

"Is Jones all right?" Thornhill asked Golay, all the built-up emotion gone from his voice.

"Yes. I called an ambulance right before I called you. I'm not a killer. I just don't trust him."

"But you trust me?" Thornhill's eyebrows angled downward as his hand made a fist.

"Who else am I going to trust?" Golay's eyes were saggy and sleepy. "I am tired of running, tired of hiding. I'm getting too old for it all. If Crumwell sent you to talk to me, then he must trust you. If we hadn't been attacked, I would have known nothing of Jones, would have told you what I know, and that would have been the end of it. I wouldn't have known about Crumwell's dishonesty."

Instead of asking questions, Thornhill, still confused, let Golay continue to talk.

"But I have lived long enough to know that the more people know about something, the more likely it will get out. Especially within an agency with moles."

Thornhill rubbed his stubbly chin. "So you think there's a mole inside my organization?"

"Of course. They have moles everywhere." Golay spoke as if this was common knowledge.

"Who are 'they'?" Thornhill had reached his limit and wanted a straight answer.

Golay looked around the boat. All the couples were so infatuated with each other, they had forgotten anyone else. This made Golay and Thornhill invisible to them. The banks of the river were littered with people walking up and down the streets or standing by the railing, watching the boats go by. Golay took out a pen from the front pouch of his bag, wrote on his hand, and then placed his hand palm up on his lap for Thornhill to see.

Thornhill looked down to see, on Golay's old, wrinkled palm, the words "The Twelve."

CHAPTER 14

ONE-STAR HOTEL

Thornhill and Golay checked into a small, rundown hotel near the highway outside Amsterdam, where teenage lovers go to lose their priceless gift, where young models have their first "photo shoot" with no knowledge of what a photographer can legally do, and where people go to hide, like Thornhill and Golay. Their room had two beds with stained bedsheets. A squat old-fashioned TV sat on top of the dresser. A dull-blue wallpaper covered the walls. To say the room was below average would be an overstatement. Golay observed the room as Thornhill checked out the bathroom.

Golay broke the silence first. "Why didn't you shoot me?"

"Let's just say I trust Crumwell more than I trust you, and he told me to listen, so that's what I'm going to do—though if you really wanted to talk to me alone, you could have passed me a note instead of shooting my partner."

Thornhill sat down on the farthest bed from the door. Golay sat across from him on the opposite bed.

"Too risky." Golay laid his bag on the bed beside him.

"But," Thornhill said, "if you trust me because Crumwell sent me, why wouldn't you trust Jones?"

"Because I know Crumwell. His concern for the safety of his agents was always his downfall. When I saw Jones, I knew Crumwell had sent him for the sole purpose of keeping you safe. Am I right?"

"That would make some sense." Thornhill was getting upset with Crumwell. Thornhill could feel Crumwell's shadow looming over him as he sat in this crummy one-star hotel room on the other side of the world. He pushed it out of his mind and proceeded to ask Golay for the truth. "The real truth, now. Your request from your letter is here, one man whom Crumwell trusts. Now, we weren't followed. This place isn't even listed on the travel sites. The rooms to both sides are empty, even though the man at the front desk chuckled at us over that. We are completely alone. So all I want is the truth. Let's start with what is in the bag."

CHAPTER 15

AN OLD MAN'S TRUTH

Golay told his story, or at least another one, while Thornhill went through the brown leather bag. The bag contained documents from several banks, with different parts highlighted or circled. At the bottom of the bag, Thornhill found an empty Colt revolver with five bullets under it, each with the words "Tall Man" engraved into the tip.

Golay's story started similarly to his lie: Janitor, NSA, and so forth. However, he added that his "friend" was Thornhill's employer, Crumwell. Because of their good friendship, Crumwell landed Golay a job as an informant over in his land of origin. From there, the story started to differ from the previous one. About a week after he got off the plane, Golay landed a job at the second-largest bank in Switzerland due to his almost perfect résumé and references. Within a month, he was promoted to head assistant accountant, a position that granted him access to almost all the bank's internal cash flow. After a year of looking into bank statements, eavesdropping on his fellow employees, and going through their offices when they were all at lunch or when he was "working late," he still had nothing. He reported back to his handler on the second Thursday of each month with the same message, "Blue," meaning he'd found nothing threatening to the United States and nothing benefiting Russia or its communist puppets.

The second year of his employment, though, something did happen. The president of the bank was a secluded man, spending most of his time in his office, not talking to anyone outside the board or his secretary. That changed. One Friday, Golay had decided to go to lunch with some of his fellow employees and see if his friendship with them could get him anything. By this time, he was about to give up on the whole mission. Golay was the last to leave for lunch. Just as the elevator doors were closing, the bank president slipped into the elevator. Golay said his greetings. The president said nothing. Golay thought it rude and stood in awkward silence with him. The president then pressed the emergency button, and the elevator stopped. Golay tensed up, his pulse racing. He feared he had been compromised. He evaluated everything he'd done, thinking of any mistakes he might have made that could have pointed the finger at him.

The president spoke without pause.

"Don't talk—listen. I know you are with the NSA. There aren't any communist funds directly tied to this bank, but there is dirty money, money so dirty that my conscience can't take it for another second. There is a group of very powerful men called The Twelve who have been laundering and hiding their money here since the end of World War II. Over the years, I have been able to find out that it has been used for many evil things. Meet me at your desk tonight at one. Here are the keys you need to get in. I'll take care of the security. Tell no one, not even your handler, of this."

The president started the elevator again and pressed the second-floor button. A few seconds later, the doors opened, and the president left as fast as he'd come in. Golay stayed in the elevator until it reached the lobby and then quietly left the building. He went about his day as usual, trying to draw little attention to himself. Once off work and home, he dropped everything near the front door and just sat on the couch with his thoughts. Under the floorboards beneath the couch was his coder, a small wooden box filled with wires under a small keyboard and an attachable antenna. His handler was waiting for a reply about now, sitting at his desk, having his early-morning coffee, chitchatting with the janitors while he waited for the message.

Golay knew if he sent "Blue," the handler's day wouldn't be any different than all the other days. He would report it, and no one would bat an eye, since nothing had changed. If Golay sent "Red," then gears would be set in motion. His superiors would wait for proof before launching an elaborate mission to, as they said, "obtain funds that are supporting antidemocratic regimes." If Golay sent "Yellow," they would then get ready for the "Red" or the "Blue" that would follow a week later. If he sent nothing for a week, he would be pre-sumed dead or rogue, all his assets would be liquidated, and a team would be sent to investigate the matter.

Golay sat there in silence for thirty minutes pondering what to do, until it hit him like a ton of bricks. He took out the coder and screwed the antenna into the top corner. He placed his fingers on the keys, about to type out "Mud." This meant there could be a mole inside the NSA. However, he paused before pressing the first key. He wondered if there actually could be a mole inside the agency. But it was the only explanation for the bank president knowing about him. The mole might hear or see the report he was about to send. Golay wondered how his report would affect the mole. Would it help him or hurt him? Golay lifted his fingers from the keys and placed them on the sides of the box while he stared at the flowered wallpaper.

He sat for another thirty minutes, trying to put himself in the mole's position. After thinking through all the possible outcomes he could create with each message if he were a mole, he came to the same solution: the mole would always have the upper hand. He slowly slid the cover of the coder back on, set it on the ground, and gazed at it. He knew the mole would have the upper hand unless Golay didn't send anything at all. At least, that's what he hoped. He put the box back in its hiding spot and went to bed, setting his alarm to wake him at eleven thirty, giving him a little time to rest before he headed back to the bank to find out the truth.

Golay dreamed that night about a Western showdown. He was the hero, of course. A tall, dark figure with white hair and a belt made out of living snakes was his nemesis.

He woke before the gunfight began. He dressed in a dark suit and a dull-white shirt, but no tie. As he was leaving, he passed his mother's room. She had gotten back from her church activities while Golay was asleep. She was lying on her side, her head on one pillow while she hugged two others, imitating the times before her better half had died. Golay slowly closed her door, quietly shoving it into place. The door would get stuck now and again. He grabbed his revolver from a hidden compartment in his desk. Grabbing his overcoat by the front door as he left, he looked back one more time with a strange feeling. He suspected it was just the butterflies in his stomach.

The drive to the bank was shorter than usual. He parked two blocks down from the bank and walked the rest of the way, checking his gun every so often, making sure the safety was off. Snow started to fall slowly as he reached the front door. The key clicked into place, and he unlocked the door. He quietly cleaned his feet on the welcome mat and walked to the elevators. Looking up at the security camera, he noted the absence of light from its little red bulb. He placed his finger on the up button and then stopped. Trying to be as quiet as he could, he turned and took the stairs. He listened carefully as he ascended. Every moment, his heart beat faster than the moment before. Golay thought his steps echoed through the staircase like a blacksmith hammering out a sword. In actuality, the sound resembled more of a mouse than a hammer.

When he reached the eighth floor, he took out the keys to the door blocking his path. As his key clicked into place, he heard a loud crack, followed by faint scream. He slowly unlocked the door and entered the floor, keeping himself as low as he could. The sound of the cracking grew louder, filling every corner of the floor. He made his way out of the hallway and into the main area. He drew his gun and carefully looked out across the cubicles. He saw no one. Another crack, followed by another shout of pain. The president's office door was open. Golay kept low and close to the wall as he passed the empty cubicles, going around them to approach the door from the side. The closer he got, the more sounds emerged from the office: the movement of a body on the floor, the whimpers of a grown man, voices. One belonged to the president, weak and frail. The other, Golay did not recognize. It had a strange accent, Slavic with hints of some South American to it. It was young, yet with a strong sense of power behind it. Golay slowly inched his way toward the door, creeping underneath a painting of the beach, listening carefully.

"Listen! Listen! Listen! I have been faithful! There is not a shred of your existence to be found in this office. I've persona—"

Another crack, followed by a yell of pain from the president. The young voice spoke in a bored tone. "Don't lie to me."

"I'm not! I swear!" Another crack, another scream.

"What did I say? Don't lie to me. We know you told someone something. Who is it?"

"All right!" The president was trying to catch his breath. "I went to a friend of mine in the police department."

"Wrong."

Another crack and another yell. Golay looked through the gap near one of the hinges to get a view of the situation. His boss—a multimillionaire, a man who had eaten dinner with the president of Switzerland on more than one occasion, who'd met Al Pacino when he had passed through, who, with the drop of a coin, could change the course of the world's economy for better or worse, who, without question, was one of the world's most powerful men—was bleeding on the ground, pleading for his life while being whipped. The person whipping him was a tall man wearing a long, brown trench coat, his hair blond and short. In his left hand, he held a seven-foot-long bullwhip, the tip dripping with blood.

"What do you want?" cried the bank president. "You already know what the truth is! Why beat me for it when you already have it?"

The tall man laughed and bent down. His voice was soft and threatening. "If we knew who it was, we would have already killed you and the agent from the NSA. However, we don't know his name or his face. So if you tell me who it is now, I'll kill you quickly and peacefully. If you don't tell me, I will pull it out of you as I pull the flesh off your bones."

The president laid his head down on the carpet, damp from his tears. He turned his head toward Golay, seeing him through the gap. He must have seen his chance for redemption, and he took it. "Two-four-eight-four-seven-one-six."

The tall man stood and went to the large painting behind the handcrafted desk. He slid the painting to the right to reveal a large safe with a dial. He dialed in the combination.

The president mouthed, "Cubicle."

Golay got up and rushed to his cubicle. He didn't account for the picture, though. He hit the beach painting he'd passed earlier. It slid to the side, hitting the wall twice but not falling off its nail. He looked up and saw the tall man look toward the office door and pull out his revolver. His right hand slowly opened the safe's door. His head was to the right of it when the explosive inside the safe went off. The door swung open with incredible force, grazing the tall man in the face, tearing skin off and breaking his cheekbone.

Golay ran straight to his cubicle and hid behind his desk. He put his hands over his mouth and sat there in silence. He looked around and saw that one of his drawers had a small plastic tab sticking out of it. A gunshot rang out. Golay peered around his desk. Footsteps echoed throughout the floor as the tall man came out of the president's office, stopping at the doorway. Blood dripped from the right side of his face, his right eye shut and half his eyebrow scraped off, leaving behind nothing but flesh and blood. He pulled out his radio.

"You all ready? Got some stuff for you all to clean up… Some trash here and there. The hard part will be the bodies… Two, only two."

The tall man quietly walked around the cubicles and spoke directly to Golay. "So, how are we going to do this?"

Golay held his breath, his heart beating faster, his hands sweating.

"Will you come to me like a good little pup? Or will I have to put you down like a sick dog?"

Golay stayed silent, pressing his finger slowly against the trigger to find resistance. His gun was ready, but he wasn't so sure about himself. The tall man had walked halfway around the cubicle space by this time. The radio beeped. Golay couldn't hear what the voice on the other end said, but what the tall man replied chilled him to the bone. "Come on. What would *she* do?"

Golay thought of his mother, and then he didn't think at all. He stood up and aimed his pistol at the tall man, who already had his own pistol, aimed at Golay, in his left hand and his radio in his right. They stood on opposite sides of the floor, light from the quarter moon pouring into the room, letting Golay see the face behind the voice. The man was younger than Golay had expected, in his early twenties, with a strong jawline and a long nose. His right eye was already swollen shut. In a better-lit room, Golay could have seen the tall man's cheekbone slightly poking out of his skin. However, in the moonlight, all Golay could see was the blood slowly dripping down the man's face.

"You ready to talk now?" the man asked.

"Are you a lefty or a righty?" Golay asked.

The man cocked back his gun with his thumb, his hand shaking slightly from the pain. He cracked a smile. "Righty."

They both fired. The man missed. Golay did not. The man took cover behind one of the cubicles, clenching his left hand as it bled. His blood covered the gun that lay beside him. Golay quickly opened his desk drawer. All his files were gone and had been replaced by a tin box. He grabbed the box and ran toward the stairs behind him.

"Don't think this is the end! I have five bullets left, and they each have your name on them!" yelled the man.

Golay swung open the staircase door and yelled back, "Ditto!"

CHAPTER 16

PAPERS FALLING

Taking back doors and alleyways, Golay was able to get a good distance between the killer and himself. He called a cab instead of returning to his car in fear someone would be watching it. He gave the cabby directions to his house. Though the cabby was reluctant to go so far, Golay offered double. After being on the road for more than half an hour, he was finally able to gain control of his nerves and calm down. However, his nerves did not stay that way. Near his house, the taxi had to pull over for two fire trucks. Golay thought nothing of it until the cab was approaching the long street he lived on. Before they turned, Golay could see that the smoke was coming from his street. He told the driver to keep on going. Though he appeared confused, the cabby kept going straight without much hesitation. Golay looked down the street as they passed. He could see, in the faint distance, two fire trucks putting out a house fire. The cab went another mile, but Golay kept staring out the window, wondering if his mother had gotten out, wondering if she was safe, wondering what to do if he lost her, wondering.

The cab driver was the first to break the silence. "Where to now?"

"I don't know." Golay looked down at the tin box on his lap. He had forgotten about the box since they'd passed his street. Golay opened it. Inside was an assortment of different bank statements, accounting balance sheets, cash flow records, the works. To the common eye, even to most accountants, it would look normal. However, Golay caught its significance. He quickly closed the box and told the driver to take him back to the city.

An hour later, in a hotel room obtained under one of his aliases, he called down to the desk to be woken up with breakfast and the morning paper at seven. Then he locked himself in and wedged a chair under the door handle. He dumped the contents of the tin box on the bed and plunged into them. By the time the sun rose, he had cross-checked each statement and report three times to discover that, through multiple money transfers between multiple accounts, millions of dollars were disappearing and reappearing, though there was no evidence of where the money was going or where it was coming from.

He pulled his gun out when he heard a knock on the door. He checked the time—7:03 a.m. He went to the door and looked through the peephole. A young maid stood in the hall with his breakfast of eggs, coffee, and toast. He opened the door and retrieved his food and newspaper. Golay figured the maid would think him rude since he closed the door in her face with no tip. But that was no matter. He went back to his bed and set his breakfast on the nightstand before again checking his work.

The morning paper fell off his tray onto the floor. He picked it up and almost tossed it back down, when he noticed the headline. A picture of his house engulfed in flames covered the front page. He quickly read through the article to find that the firefighters had been able to stop the blaze, which had had the possibility of starting a wildfire. The article went on to say that a broken gas line and faulty wiring had caused half the house to blow up and had set the rest on fire. One death was reported, an elderly woman, found in her bedroom, burned to death.

The paper slipped through Golay's hands and hit the ground with a light thud. Golay didn't hear it, though. Tears filled his eyes. He placed his head in his hands and wept. Guilt, grief, regret, and pain swept through his body all at once, but the dominant emotion was anger. He grabbed the pillow next to him, and like a small child, he screamed into it at the top of his lungs. Every cuss word he knew, in three different languages, came out of his mouth.

He continued in that fashion for an hour until he had used up all his energy. He lowered the pillow from his face and looked around, his eyes puffy from his tears. He saw the bank papers surrounding his bed, each the cause of his mother's death. He saw the tin box sitting beside him, empty as a coffin before the dead person is placed inside. Golay grabbed it and threw it against the wall behind him. The box cracked in half as the corner of it hit the wall. It left a hole in the wall the size of a child's hand. Golay cussed under his breath.

He looked at the two pieces of what had been a tin box and thought about how they, coincidently, imitated his life at the moment, in pieces. He noticed a note sticking out of the bottom of one half of the box. He picked up the piece with the note. There was a small compartment hidden in the box, just big enough for a couple of letters. It was there the note had been hidden. There was no way, except by breaking the box, that Golay could ever have found the note. He pulled out the note…and found the hidden account.

CHAPTER 17

TRUTH AND JUSTICE

Golay stood up from his chair and walked to the bed. Opening a secret compartment in the bottom of his messenger bag, he pulled out the documents he'd spoken of and gave them to Thornhill. As he flipped through the pages, Thornhill could smell the old musk of forty years. They were typed records of an account by the name of The Twelve. Thornhill could understand them, somewhat. What really caught his eye was the handwritten note card from Golay's boss. All it gave was an address and a time in Amsterdam.

"I take it this was why you went to Amsterdam?" asked Thornhill.

"What else was I going to do? My cover was blown by an enemy I hadn't even heard of, my mother was killed, and my home was burned to the ground. What other choice did I have?"

"You could have dropped it. Left it behind you and started a new life. Yet you didn't. Why?"

Golay's gaze fell to the floor. His forehead wrinkled, and his cheeks puffed up with air before he slowly let it out. "Curiosity." Lifting his head with a tilt toward Thornhill, he added, "Truth, justice, revenge. Those would be the main reasons."

"Is that why you chased after The Twelve all these years? You were curious?"

Golay chuckled. "No. Curiosity only lasts for so long. The older you get, the more you see the meaninglessness in revenge. Truth and justice brought me a long way. Not far enough, though."

Thornhill could see an emptiness filling Golay's eyes as he gazed into the distance, the gaze of a man handing off his life's purpose, a man who wouldn't live to see the results of his actions.

"What do you mean truth?" asked Thornhill. "I mean, I get justice, bringing punishment to those who have done evil. But what about truth? What is truth?"

Golay had a blank stare on his face for a few seconds before giving his response. "It's what really happened. It's what happened at a certain moment that will never change no matter how many people ignore it, deny it, or hide it. It happened, so it became the truth of that moment. People can have opinions of the truth, and those opinions can change over time, but truth doesn't change."

"And the truth you're looking for is that of this organization named The Twelve?" asked Thornhill.

"Yes."

"So, back to the story. Does it change that much from the earlier lie?"

"No, it's just a little duller. There was no girl. Well… yes and no. I saw her at the same place we met. However, I didn't approach her, for obvious reasons. But I have never seen such a beautiful girl since then."

"Creeper," said Thornhill in a sarcastic tone.

Golay cracked a smile and then laughed. "If you saw her, you would think differently."

"Oh, I understand. I just wouldn't chicken out." They both laughed.

"Well, maybe if I wasn't a spy, I may have done something about it."

"Great spies are lonely spies."

"Got that right."

"So, how did the rest of your trip in Amsterdam go?"

"Well, it was uneventful, until the day I got the note card I spoke of. I went early to find the pier and hid under it until after sunset. That's when they came. It took place like I told you, excluding the death, and the tall man was there, which just confirmed everything more. The rest of the story is the same."

Thornhill wasn't satisfied with the truth Golay presented, though his opinion didn't change the matter. That was all Golay had seen and heard. What relevance it had to a threat to the United States was up to Thornhill.

"Why did you contact Crumwell?" asked Thornhill.

"When I was running around Europe after I lost my cover, I sent a letter to Crumwell telling him I was onto something, something big. I didn't give him details, just told him to meet me a year from that day. He used his vacation days to get away. It wasn't hard to find him. When we met up, I gave him photocopies of what I had gotten, which at the time was barely enough to convince him, but it did. He told me what happened at the agency. My handler was transferred to South America, and they said I was dead. A car wreck, or some accident like that. He said he would keep his ear to the ground and told me to lie low. He gave me a new ID just in case they were getting close, and we decided to both gather as much information on them as we could."

"And you found what you were looking for and wanted to inform Crumwell of it? And when he sends two agents instead of himself, you panic and shoot one?" asked Thornhill in a calm and quiet voice, no anger in his words, just assumptions.

Golay looked at Thornhill, his face stern but his eyes tired. "When you've spent a lifetime looking over your shoulder for an enemy you can't see or fully understand, you become a little paranoid." Golay sniffled. Thornhill offered him a tissue from the box on the nightstand. Golay blew his nose and said, "I'm tired, and what I know needs to be passed down to someone who will use it to bring them down."

"But why trust me and not Jones?" asked Thornhill sincerely.

"Because Crumwell trusts you with secrets and trusts Jones to protect you."

Thornhill was pondering that statement when Golay added, "If they hadn't tried to kill us, I would have told you everything and told you not to tell a soul. Hopefully you wouldn't have, and I would have walked away to a new life, but that didn't happen…Missions hardly ever go as planned."

"You're telling me. So, what did you find?"

CHAPTER 18

No Choice

Jones lay still in a hospital bed, having some of the most peaceful nights of his life. His wound was not life threatening. The police didn't bother him much, only questioning him once. He told lies well. He informed them he was just touring through Europe, staying at cheap hotels. He'd heard a knock on his door. Unknowingly, he had opened the door to a masked man with a gun. It all went blank after that, according to him.

No operation was needed, as the bullet had passed straight through him. The nurse said he would be out in a couple of weeks. Jones saw it as a paid vacation. The American TV programs that were available were decent, and he still had his books, since they'd brought his things from his hotel room. Nothing incriminating in them. He knew it wouldn't take long for Glass to locate him. Then he would be on his way back home. He hoped Thornhill was wiser than he was. He hoped Thornhill wouldn't trust Golay. He hoped Thornhill was still alive.

As he slept the second night at the hospital, he dreamt of nothing but the sun and the forest as he wandered its endless trails. It was the first time since his military tour that he didn't dream about Iraq and his mistakes. As he sat in the forest of his mind and enjoyed the beauty of it, he heard the faint sound of his name on the wind. He stood up. Listening closely, he heard it again, this time sounding like distant thunder. The third time, it was like lightning, awakening him from his slumber. His eyes opened to see his hospital room filled with six police officers, two at the door, one closing the shades, and two standing at the end of his bed. The sixth one sat beside him, calling his name. Jones turned his head to get a better look at the officer beside him.

"Hello, Jones, welcome back." The policeman's face was old, his white hair cut short like a soldier's, and half his right eyebrow was missing.

"I'm sorry. I'm not Jones. I'm Taylor, Jack Taylor." Jones's voice was groggy. He would stick to his lie to the end, however close that may be.

"Jones, I really don't want to play games." The officer pulled out a small black box and opened it to reveal three syringes. Two were filled with a clear liquid, while the other was empty.

Jones tried to tense up his muscles, readying them for the fight ahead, but his body did nothing. He attempted to grab his sheets, kick his legs, move his fingers, or wiggle his toes, any type of movement. Nothing. His body stayed as still as a corpse. Jones's heartbeat rose.

"Medicine is an amazing thing, is it not? Now, I'm not a doctor of any sort, but I have some extremely talented friends who are." The officer leaned on the bed, making sure Jones could see the needles. "Now I don't know how my friends did it, but they made up a serum that, when ejected right, will numb the whole body, except the head." He pointed to the empty syringe. "Now, do you want to take a guess at what these do?" He pointed to the other two syringes. Jones had an idea, though he wished he hadn't.

"Some sort of truth-telling serum?"

The officer chuckled. "I actually have no clue. They just told me to use them if I ever wanted anyone to suffer. See, I never saw what would happen, but I remember passing their labs and hearing the screams from the pigs and the dogs and the monkeys they would use to test it on." The officer shook his head. "It was a haunting sound. Though you've heard worse, I presume, being in Iraq and all."

Jones gave no reaction.

The officer leaned back in his chair, taking Jones's phone out of his pocket and spinning it between his fingers. "The sound of those men. I mean, if I was in your position, I would have let the kid go as well. But to leave your post at night and double-cross your whole squad to a bunch of terrorists just to make sure you got out alive…" The officer nodded in appreciation. "Pretty clever. Though I think the best part wasn't when you took their dog tags and planted them on some burned bodies in the middle of the desert. No, the best part, in my eyes, the part that made us consider you as an agent, was when you shot yourself in the leg with an enemy's gun and crawled back to your base, playing the part of an escaped prisoner of war perfectly."

Jones held back tears with all his might and choked out, "I had no choice."

The officer hushed Jones and continued his speech. "You see, with that kind of brilliance, you could have easily been brought into our organization. However, we have zero tolerance for traitors. So, why don't you do what you do best and tell me everything."

CHAPTER 19

THE EIGHTH FLOOR

Thornhill woke up past dinnertime. That didn't bother him, though. Golay was still asleep in the other bed when Thornhill went into the bathroom. He took a shower and dressed in a dark-gray dinner suit—no tie—and black dress shoes. He gathered his belongings from his suitcase: chrome watch, leather wallet, false passport, Glock 9 mm with armor-piercing rounds and silencer, and an envelope containing eighteen thousand euros. He felt around the end of his suitcase for a little bump. He slid the bump to the seam in the lining. He tore a small hole in the lining with a pen and took out a small box, no bigger than the tip of his pinky finger. Inside was a small tracking bug nestled in foam padding. He closed the box and placed it in his inside jacket pocket. He pulled out his phone, took off the back of it, and removed what looked like a SIM card, though in reality it was a one-way receiver synced to his cell phone's earpiece. He placed the bug in the inside pocket of his suit and left quietly, leaving the Do Not Disturb sign on the door.

He hailed a cab. Once inside the taxi, Thornhill took out his cell phone. He stared at it for a moment, pondering whether he should turn it on to let Mallory know where he was. He gazed out the window, catching glimpses of the sun setting through the new and old buildings all smashed together like a panini sandwich. The cab came to a stop. Thornhill didn't bother to look at where they were. He just stared out the window, looking past the people walking the streets, until he saw her. A blond woman, probably in her midtwenties, wearing a two-piece pinstriped suit. She reminded him of Mallory to some extent. It wasn't because of her stance, and her idiosyncrasies weren't even close to Mallory's. Her eyes weren't even the same color, but the hair was. All it took was that blond hair to bring Mallory to his mind.

He looked at his cell phone and mulled over the conversation he'd had with Golay. He slid the phone back into his pocket. Thornhill knew if Golay was right, there could be a chance a mole was still present in Glass. It would account for the attack at the coffee shop. Thornhill stopped himself there. He knew once the thought of a mole was introduced, no one was safe from suspicion. He focused his mind on the now: collect information, find Jones, and get home safely.

The cab pulled up to the InterContinental Amstel Amsterdam Hotel. As Thornhill approached the front door, he was flabbergasted by its beauty. Its nineteenth-century style mixed well with the modernizing city, standing next to the Amstel River as if it were the one dictating where the river should flow. The white accents of the windows popped against the dark tan bricks covering the building. During the day, the sky-blue rooftop would melt almost perfectly into the clear blue sky above it. Thornhill wouldn't have trouble seeing the hotel that night. Like a prized treasure in a museum, Amsterdam lit up the Amstel. The Dutch flag flew high, with the flags of Amsterdam and the Amstel under it. As Thornhill entered the building, a polished wooden staircase greeted him, ascending half a story before splitting in two directions to lead to the second floor. A dull-golden flowered rug covered the middle of the stairs. A golden sun clock hung at the end of the hall, and it peered through the white arches that stood above the staircase like a noonday sun, ticking down to its setting. After checking in with his fake ID, Thornhill retrieved his key card and then went back to the front entrance and approached a valet.

"Good evening, sir, how may I help you?" asked the valet. He was in his late twenties, and though he sounded cheerful, his voice told Thornhill he had been going through the motions for many years.

"I'm doing well, though I seem to have lost my friend, and I'm already late for a meeting. Do you think you can call my room the instant you see him? You don't need to stop him. Here is a picture of him with my room number on the back." Thornhill handed him a small picture of Fredrick with a twenty-euro bill behind it.

The valet took the photo and the money. "Of course, sir," he responded with a smile.

"Thank you."

Thornhill left the valet and went to the bar. Dark wood surrounded the lounge, and there were oil paintings and small marble statues sprinkled around. Entrepreneurs, politicians, and ambassadors in suits and dresses were everywhere, along with high-priced escorts of both genders. Most were in small groups, one consisting of old men talking about the global economic crisis, blaming the Americans for it. A younger man surrounded by women talked of his great achievements in the world of politics. Their interest was as big as his pocketbook. Another group spoke of the Middle East, while the one next to them talked of past World Cups.

Thornhill then spotted what he was looking for—an elderly woman and a younger man sat at the bar, talking. She was going through her purse, taking out her car keys to get her credit card, when the man suggested they continue their conversation in her room. She agreed, and they started to walk toward Thornhill through the light crowd. She hung her purse from her arm by one strap, while the other one dangled. Thornhill started walking toward the bar, his left hand in his pocket and his right hand free. As they passed each other, Thornhill gently grazed her side as he slipped two fingers into her purse and retrieved her keys. His two years in Xian as a teen came back like an old habit. A good spy must know how to pickpocket. Where better to learn that skill than in the city of thieves?

Thornhill went to the bathroom and stayed in a stall for two minutes before washing his hands and leaving the bar. The couple had already left, but he would rather play it safe. Thornhill took the elevator to the eighth floor. His hands grew clammy. Reaching into his inside pocket, he pulled out the small box. He took out the tracker, pulling off the protective plastic as if he were peeling open a Band-Aid. Lifting a small lever on one side, he shoved it under the fingernail of his left middle finger. The elevator reached its destination. Thornhill walked to his room, his mind playing out all the worst possible scenarios if things went bad. He took out his key card and entered room 972. Fredrick greeted Thornhill at the door, shoving his sweat-covered handkerchief into his jacket pocket.

"Mr. Smith! So glad you could make it! I hope your day went well?"

Thornhill shook Fredrick's hand, placing his left hand on the man's shoulder. "It was better with this night in sight. Nice suit. Where did you get it?"

Fredrick glanced down at himself, trying to hide his pride. "This old thing? My tailor made it up a couple of weeks ago."

Thornhill didn't even need to hear that to know it was a lie. The suit didn't fit Fredrick at all. The sleeves were a quarter inch too short, and the pants were about an inch too long. The fabric was secondhand, probably a couple of years old. Thornhill played along, though, feeling the collar of the jacket with his left hand, placing the tracker under the collar and breaking off the lever to turn the device on. "You must give me his name sometime," he said.

"He's a very picky man when it comes to his customers, but I think I could get you in."

Thornhill could smell the pride wafting off Fredrick like rotten blue cheese. He kept his face impassive, nodding in response.

"Well, would you like to meet the girls?"

"That is why I'm here." Thornhill knew the hardest part was over already. He just had to play along until Fredrick took his leave. He was led through a small sitting area into the bedroom. A king-sized bed with soft yellow sheets sat in the middle of the caramel-colored room. A lamp with a red lampshade on the nightstand beside the bed gave the room a calm, autumnal feel, though that was not the true state of the room—not with three girls sitting on the bed. The sixteen-year-old blonde sat between a redhead and brunette, both of whom had experienced their fifteenth birthday a week earlier. The redhead wore a white summer dress that almost matched her pale skin, while the brunette wore a short pink dress that matched her bright-pink lipstick. The blonde towered over the two other girls. Her purple-striped black dress wrapped around her tightly, squeezing her like a tube of toothpaste. Their makeup was fresh, though their eyes were puffy from crying. Thornhill tried not to think about how Fredrick and his men had caught the girls, though he had an idea about how they'd "persuaded" them. Fredrick started to introduce them, but Thornhill stopped him.

"I will learn their names on my own, but you have truly outdone yourself, Fredrick."

As Thornhill walked him to the door, Fredrick puffed out his chest and said, "If you have any traveling friends who are looking for a good time, just give them my name."

"I will indeed, though I don't think any of them are coming through Amsterdam soon, so it may be a while."

"Well, if they are coming through Europe, I can still hook them up."

Thornhill raised an eyebrow, his surprise the truest emotion he'd shown that whole night. "Really? You have some partners?"

Fredrick chuckled. "I guess you could say that."

Thornhill didn't push the matter. He didn't want to raise suspicion. "In that case, I will definitely give them your name."

A greedy smile spread across Fredrick's face as he stepped out of the room. "Glad to hear it. I will inform my partners about your friends."

Thornhill handed Fredrick an envelope containing eighteen thousand euros. The two men discussed when Fredrick would come to pick up the girls the next day, and then they said their good-byes. Thornhill closed the door and peeped through the peephole to see Fredrick counting the money. He tucked it in his pocket and walked cheerfully out of Thornhill's sight.

Thornhill went to the bedroom to see the girls still seated on the bed, unmoved but not untouched. Thornhill ignored them and went straight to the window. He looked at his watch and pulled one of the three dials as he pushed another in. The hands stopped telling time and pointed to where the tracker was and how far away it was. His phone rang. It was the valet informing him that his friend had just left the building and was hailing a cab. Thornhill said nothing and hung up. He pulled up a chair in front of the girls. They trembled in fear as he sat there in silence for a couple of seconds, though to them it must have felt like hours.

"Were you all kidnapped?"

They shook their heads in small movements.

"Are you all in debt to them?"

They nodded yes.

"Are you all from here?"

They shook their heads again.

"From Germany?"

They nodded.

Thornhill was surprised that Fredrick had told him the truth about the girls. "Where were you before they brought you here?"

They stayed silent.

"Did you even know where you were?"

They shook their heads.

Thornhill stroked his chin, sighed, and decided he had hit a dead end. He reached into his pocket and pulled out three thousand euros and gave them to the blond girl, leaving him two thousand euros for the rest of the mission. "Don't go to the police," he told the girls. "Wait here for a couple of minutes and then go straight to the train station and take the next train back home. Got it?"

They nodded in understanding.

Thornhill had gotten up to walk out the door, when the blond girl stopped him, standing up and saying, "Wait, can you walk us to the train?" Her eyes pleaded for help, but Thornhill didn't have the time. Glancing at his watch, he saw that the distance between him and Fredrick was growing.

"I'm sorry. I can't. I have to go to catch the people who did this to you. Take a cab to the train station, walk in the light, stay in public places, and you will be fine. By this time tomorrow, you all will be back with your parents."

She lowered her head with a soft "OK."

"Chin up," Thornhill said, leaning his head under hers to see her eyes. "The nightmare is almost over."

She lifted her head and gave a small smile. Thornhill smiled back a bigger smile and left them.

When he reached the front of the hotel, he handed the keys he'd stolen to the valet, a younger one than the first. A couple of minutes passed, and then the valet returned in a white Bentley Continental GT V-8. Thornhill tipped the valet and settled into the dark-gray leather seats of the Bentley. Smooth jazz played over the sound system as he adjusted the seat to his liking while driving to Fredrick's safe haven. He followed only his watch for guidance and drove for thirty minutes, the city slowly changing around him. The modern, well-kept buildings faded into the canals as graffiti grew like weeds on the rundown buildings. He passed an empty square that earlier that morning had been filled with farmers and craftsmen, selling their goods to local residents and a few adventurous tourists.

He parked near an unnamed avenue, his watch informing him it was the last turn. He turned the car off, took out a pair of latex gloves from his wallet, and put them on. Pulling his gun out, he checked the clip, turned off the safety, and screwed on the silencer. He got out of the car and walked down the alley that ran parallel to the street, sneaking from trash bin to doorway, making sure no residents saw him. Four blocks down the alley, his watch informed him that he had reached his destination by pointing all its hands to twelve o'clock. An old red brick building stood before him. A broken fire escape ascended from the second floor to the eighth floor. There was a faded green door under it, surrounded by an archway of brick sticking out from the rest of the wall. It was enough for Thornhill.

He slowly climbed onto the archway, holding on to a second-story window to keep his balance as he reached for the fire escape. His average height prevented him from reaching it. He bent his legs a bit, keeping his eyes off his feet and on the metal ladder hanging down from the fire escape, and jumped. The metal ladder swung with his weight and made a loud clanging sound. He quickly pulled himself up and climbed onto the fire escape. Once there, he put his back against the wall and waited. It was quiet for a couple of minutes. Then he heard a window open about two stories above him. Thornhill held his breath so its plume, in the cold air, would not be seen. Seconds passed before he heard the window close.

He quietly resumed his climb, tiptoeing up the metal staircase, pulling his gun out in case things went south. Each window he passed, he checked for any hints of Fredrick. Most windows only looked down dirty and empty hallways filled with beer bottles, used condoms, and needles. He saw few people. One floor had a couple of girls smoking and talking about their last clients. Two floors above that were a couple of men carrying a girl out of a room, her body limp in their arms. Thornhill waited until they descended the staircase before he continued. When he reached the eighth floor, he heard a loud crack and knew he was too late.

CHAPTER 20

THE WHIMPERS OF A PIMP

Fredrick was gagged, handcuffed to a cheap wooden bed, and lying face down on the floor as the tall man whipped his bare back. The tall man fit Golay's description well, just older and with some wrinkles. He wore a long raincoat, its color similar to chocolate milk. Half of his right eyebrow was missing.

"All right, one more time, Aldert. Why is he alive?" said the tall man, releasing his tired voice from the confines of his lungs.

Fredrick tried to yell through the gag, tears streaking down his face, but only loud murmurs exited his mouth.

"I know they failed, but Fredrick, they were your men, and they made a big mess, a mess I had to clean up. And if you look back on the past, where has the glory fallen? The bonuses? The fresh women? The fresh boys? Where did it all fall?"

Fredrick closed his eyes, murmuring a word. The tall man leaned against the bed, his back toward the window.

"That's right. It fell on you. So where do you think the blame should fall with failure?"

Fredrick pressed his head against the corner of the bed and whispered his answer.

"What?" the tall man asked, kneeling down to hear him better.

Fredrick mumbled it again, turning his face away in shame.

"That's right," said the tall man, and he gave Fredrick a heavy pat on the back.

Fredrick let out a muffled scream of pain.

"It does fall on you. So that's why you must be punished. Because in this business, we can't afford any mistakes or loose ends." The tall man stood up, took out a handkerchief with his bullet-scarred left hand, and wiped Fredrick's blood off his hand. "And Aldert, you're one of them." He drew his gun and pointed it at the back of Fredrick's head.

Fredrick shoved his face into his shoulder, trying to hide from his impending doom. The tall man cocked his revolver.

Thornhill took his aim with his gun, his breathing slowing. A minute of silence passed. The faint sound of sex and rap music could be heard from the floors below as Fredrick cried silently.

"Then again." The tall man took the gun away from Fredrick's head and looked at it. "I could save a bullet and let you bleed to death."

Thornhill lowered his gun but kept it at the ready.

"That could send a nice message to your replacement, don't you think?" The tall man chuckled to himself and

THE JANITOR AND THE SPY

gave Fredrick a final farewell as he left. "Good-bye, Aldert Fredrick. I hope your replacement is wiser then you."

With that, the tall man left the room. Thornhill patiently waited a couple of minutes, listening to Fredrick's weeping, and then slowly opened the window and entered the room. Fredrick was still on the floor, making no effort to get out of his handcuffs. He lay motionless, accepting his fate. One would think he was dead if not for the whimpering sounds he was making. Thornhill quickly glanced around the room for the handcuff keys but couldn't see them. He knelt beside Fredrick, reassuring him as he tried to figure out how to get him out of this predicament.

"Don't talk. I'll get you out of here," he said.

"No, you can't! No one can!" groaned Fredrick, bursting into tears again.

Thornhill helped him to his knees. Fredrick leaned his shoulder on the bedframe. It seemed there was no end to his tears. Thornhill tried to comfort him while still looking around the room for the keys. He kept his ears open for anything that sounded like Fredrick's men wanting to find out what their boss was crying about, but he heard nothing except the whimpers of a pimp.

"It's going to be OK," Thornhill said. "I'm going to get you out of here and to a hospital, and y—"

"It won't matter! They will find me! No one can escape them!" Fredrick was trying to yell at the top of his lungs, but his voice came out weak and breathless.

"Who? Who are they, Fredrick? Who are they?"

"They will kill me! There's no way out!"

Thornhill grabbed Fredrick's face, holding his eyelids open with his thumbs, making Fredrick look at him. "Fredrick, Fredrick! Look at me! Who are you talking about? What's their name?"

"I don't know. Joe never said their name."

Thornhill loosened his grip. "Is that the tall man's name? Joe?"

Fredrick nodded.

Thornhill knew he couldn't get anything from that. "Why did you do it?"

Fredrick was silent, considering the question for a second. The pimp's sweaty pallor and the amount of blood he was losing told Thornhill that he didn't have much time to get the answers he needed.

"I don't know. Money—sex, maybe. I was just the next dude in line, I guess. Shit! I shouldn't have left America!"

Thornhill took Fredrick's pulse. It was rapid but weak. Thornhill knew he could get a couple of more answers out of the pimp before he went unconscious. After that, he would have about ten minutes before he was dead. Thornhill had to choose his next questions wisely.

"Fredrick—stay with me, Fredrick—how did he contact you?"

"At a pay phone two blocks south of here."

"Did he ever meet you in person before this?"

"No, our meetings were all over the phone, damn it! Why did I sleep with her?"

He was fading fast. Thornhill could hear footsteps coming up the stairs, the cleanup crew he'd predicted.

"Fredrick! Who's the next in line?"

"James, James George, a Brit. A good fellow, better than me, better than me. Why did I do it? I shouldn't have killed the puppy!"

He was gone. His eyes started to roll back in his head as he continued to mumble nonsense, a result of shock going into full swing. Thornhill lowered Fredrick's unconscious head back onto the floor. The footsteps had now reached the door. The doorknob turned, and two thugs walked in.

CHAPTER 21

THE OVEN

James George walked into his old boss's room. Fredrick lay on the floor, unconscious and bleeding out. Jeff, George's right-hand man, gagged at the sight of the blood.

"Come on, man. Grow a spine!" snapped George. "Did you get that shower curtain? Hand it here." George took one of the shower curtains Jeff was carrying and proceeded to slowly wrap the body in it, trying to hold back his own disgust. "Well? Help me!" barked George. Jeff then followed suit, helping him wrap the body. Fredrick exhaled as they rolled him into the third layer of shower curtain. They both stopped in their tracks, staring at the body and then at each other.

"Is he still alive?" asked Jeff.

"No…that's just the oxygen left in his lungs escaping," replied George hesitantly. Though George had shot a couple of men in his time, he had never stayed to take care of the remains.

They quickly finished wrapping up the fat man in shower curtains, using duct tape to keep them from unwrapping. Jeff grabbed the legs as George lifted the head. Fredrick's face was barely visible through the plastic. George ignored the chills down his spine and kept his eyes forward as they carried Fredrick out the door. George stopped short of the door when he heard a sound behind him. He quickly looked behind him and surveyed the room. A closed window, a bloodstained bedpost, a partly open closet, and a rusty metal cabinet were the only things he saw.

"Why did you stop?" asked Jeff.

"Get someone to check the room," George whispered. Obeying orders, Jeff kicked the wall. A second later, a thug appeared from one of the side rooms down the hall. He had no shirt on and was wearing blue jeans and a belt with a huge buckle of an eagle. Jeff whispered to him to check the room.

The thug looked startled at what they were carrying, but he grabbed his gun and squeezed by them to get into the room as they descended down the hallway toward the stairs. The thug slowly approached the closet, his sawed-off shotgun ready. Placing his hand on the doorknob of the closet, he jerked it open, only to reveal a closet full of clothes. He chuckled to himself as he closed the door, relieved, mocking George and his paranoia. He opened the window and looked up and down, seeing nothing but the blackness of the alley surrounding the building. His senses were calming down from seeing his boss dead. His thoughts wandered to his payday and the new group of girls who were coming in that Friday. He knelt down, putting his gun on the bed to check under it.

After about twenty minutes, eight flights of stairs, and several breaks, Jeff and George finally got the obese body to the bottom floor. They would have used the elevator, but it had been broken for almost a year now, and no one wanted to pay to fix it. They carried the cooling corpse into the kitchen. This building had been a pizza parlor back in its earlier days, before the red lights started to come on and the families stopped coming, forcing the quiet little pizza place to sell.

George and Jeff squeezed through the steel sinks and vacant cupboards and headed toward the brick oven. They slid the body into it, laying it snugly against the logs that were already inside. They closed the door and turned on the oven. Before long, the body started to burn and stink up the kitchen. George went out back to make sure the vent from the oven was open. It was. The smell wasn't as strong outside as it was inside. George stood there in the back alley, the only light coming from the bulb above the door behind him. He gazed up at the sky, seeing only a couple of stars through the smoke and ashes of his former boss. He took a deep sigh and muttered to himself, "That won't be me. That won't be me."

"You're right," said a voice behind him.

George felt his legs give way. The butt of a pistol shoved his head down toward the ground, but he was stopped short by his arm being held straight behind him, twisted to its brink. His resisted his first instinct to scream, feeling the barrel of the gun at the back of his head.

"When and where are you meeting Joe?" demanded Thornhill.

"Four thirty this morning at the pay phone two blocks south of here! I'm supposed to answer on the third ring!"

This matched up with what Fredrick had said. Thornhill twisted George's wrist to see his watch—3:50 a.m.

"Will he ever meet you in person?"

"Yes, but on his terms, which usually aren't good."

It made some sense to Thornhill. If a bigger company wanted to keep tabs on a smaller, external part, it would limit its contact as much as possible.

"How do they get their share of the money?"

"I don't know, man. I was just a grunt."

Thornhill shoved his knee into George's back, smashing his face to the ground and twisting his shoulder farther, making small tears in his shoulder muscles.

"How do they get their money?"

"I don't know. I don't know!" George squealed in pain, his other arm hammering the ground.

"Take a guess?" Thornhill relieved some pressure from George's arm. He slowed his whimpering.

"They may have gotten it from the ATM."

Thornhill detected no sarcasm in George's voice, so he repressed his instinct to break the man's arm. "What ATM?"

"That's how Fredrick would launder the money. It always seemed like he came back with a little less than he left with, but he always told me I just counted wrong."

"Where is the last ATM you used?" Thornhill knew they wouldn't use the same ATM twice in a row, because he wouldn't have, either.

"The bridge south of here, between the drugstore and the little Asian restaurant. Please don't kill me, man!"

This caused Thornhill to pause. George's eyes were closed, a tear ran down his face, and he was whispering "Please" over and over again.

Thornhill leaned in and whispered in his ear, "Not yet."

CHAPTER 22

A Broken Tile

George woke up on the kitchen floor. His shoulder felt dislo-cated. He grabbed the steel counter and pulled himself up, only to almost fall again due to his head feeling heavier than a bowling ball as it throbbed like a drum. He bent over the counter and got his thoughts together. He lifted his head and saw a bottle of pain pills and a clock beside them reading 4:17 a.m. He grabbed the nearby sink, splashed some water on his face, and took a couple of pain pills for his head. He pat-ted himself down, making sure he didn't have his cell phone on him, as directed. He ran out of the building and headed south toward the pay phone. Five minutes later, he reached his destination. He stood quietly beside the pay phone for the next couple of minutes, checking his cheap watch every ten seconds. He observed his surroundings. No one was in sight. Only the light of the stars and a streetlamp kept him company.

His heart stopped when the phone rang. His thin hand reached for it, but he stopped himself and waited for the third ring. A second ring echoed down the empty city street. It seemed like an eternity before the third ring. When it came, George felt a great wave of relief and fear rush over him as he picked up the phone to hear an old man's voice at the other end. The voice of the man known as Joe.

CHAPTER 23

WARM MILK

"Under your feet is a loose tile. Please lift it up and take the file under it." Joe spoke into the hotel phone while sitting on a bed with white bedsheets. He was wearing flannel pajamas and sipping warm milk. A copy of the file he had left for George lay on the bed beside him. He heard George searching for the file. Another file about Golay and descriptions of his activities also lay on Joe's bed beside a map of Amsterdam. Jones's cell phone was on the ground, connected to a little black box. Joe pored over the files while waiting for George. Joe wondered where Golay was, wishing he'd gotten more information from Jones.

"The one right under me?" stammered George.

Joe knew George was new, so he gave him a little slack. "Yes. A crack in the corner should allow you to lift it up with ease."

"Well, I did, but nothing is there."

Joe stopped what he was doing and took a small plastic bag full of old cell phones with Post-it notes on them out of the nightstand. He took out the one marked P4D.

"George, did you see a police officer on your way over there?"

Joe heard George sneeze and the sound of him stepping on a glass bottle—or that's what Joe thought it was. George didn't answer his question.

"George?" Joe asked. He sent a text to his contact in P4D. He slowly put the cell phone down and gave his full attention to his hotel phone. He then heard the sound of light breathing on the other end of the phone, and he knew. He proceeded to ask one more question, for he knew the person on the other end would answer, no matter what he wanted. "Where?"

"Seven o'clock, the Czech pier."

CHAPTER 24

AN OLD-FASHIONED DUEL

Golay sat at the end of the pier in one of the two fold-up chairs he had brought along with a small plastic table, upon which rested a brown paper bag. He was smoking a cigar and watching the sun rise from the sea. Its golden light reflected off the sea back into the sky. Golay heard footsteps behind him, slowly approaching.

"Beautiful view, isn't it?" Golay asked the footsteps. They stopped. A deep breath followed, and then an older version of the same voice that had cursed Golay that day so many years ago.

"I've seen better," said Joe, sitting down in the empty chair beside Golay.

"I take it I'm surrounded."

"Can't take any chances with a dangerous man like you."

"I'm flattered." Golay took another puff of his cigar and slowly exhaled, savoring the flavor and the burn.

"What's in the bag?" inquired Joe.

Golay stuck his cigar in his mouth, opened the bag, took out a revolver by its barrel, and placed it on top of the bag. Joe picked it up and slipped out a bullet. There was something written on it: "Tall Man." Joe pulled his own gun from his holster and gave a single bullet to Golay so he could read his name on the bullet.

Golay gave the bullet back to Joe as he placed his gun back on the plastic table. They both chuckled about the situation.

"I guess we both weren't joking about it that night," said Golay.

"Apparently not." Joe laughed. "How much do you want?"

"You think money will solve this?"

Joe took a moment before giving Golay an answer. "Yes."

Golay chuckled. "Well, that is where you and I differ."

"Then why did you want me here?"

"I have some questions."

"I have some, too. An answer for an answer?"

Golay sat in silence, looking out across the sea to give the impression he was thinking hard about the question, but he knew Joe could see through his charade.

"Why not?" Golay laid his cigar on the table and folded his hands on his lap. "Who will go first?"

"I will." Joe leaned forward in his chair. "Who sent the agent?"

Golay laughed and lied. "There was no agent. I set it all up to stir things up a bit, cause a little trouble, not panic, but concern. My turn." Golay paused, not to get an idea of what to ask but of what lie to tell next, and Joe probably knew this. "Is your organization a global one?"

"Yes."

Golay was hoping for some elaboration on this answer, but before he knew it, Joe was asking his next question. Golay wondered if Joe was trying to find hidden truths in the midst of the lies. "Why do you want to stir things up?"

"To find out who worked for you and to see if what I got from them was of any value."

"So you do want money?" asked Joe.

"Not yet. My turn. How do you all make money?"

"Many different ways. The main three, though, are drugs, guns, and sex. What did you learn?"

Golay sat back in his chair and puffed out his chest. "Well, I can't tell you that." He picked up his cigar and took a puff.

"Oh, come on. I'll tell you what I learned."

"You are going to tell me what I just told you?" Golay chuckled and Joe joined him.

"No," said Joe, "what Jones told me."

Golay dropped his cigar. It bounced off the pier and into the ocean.

Joe continued, "It didn't take long to break him, him being in that kind of condition. The bullet went straight through him, ripping his lung in half. A painful sight to see. He's at peace now. To think he came to help you, and your response was to shoot him. We made you quite paranoid."

"What did you find out?" Golay asked in a somber voice.

"Well, most likely nothing like what you got about us from a pimp off the streets of Amsterdam, but I thought it was pretty interesting. Swiss accounts, files, Glass, Crumwell. But what was really interesting was his cell phone. Quite advanced. I sent it up the line and should be able to hear back about it relatively soon. I am impressed with Crumwell's ability to keep secrets. Our agents didn't know anything about this failed mission, though they will have wished they had." Joe visibly relaxed back in his chair, and Golay knew Joe had trumped him with his king. "Anyways, your turn." Joe didn't know, though, that Golay had one more card in his hand, but even Golay wasn't sure if it was an ace or a deuce.

"No." He would play it like an ace and hope for the best.

"So, are we done here?" Joe placed his hands on the folding chair's arms.

"Yes." Golay released his breath as if it was his last.

"Good. Also, you can keep the files you have as a souvenir. We don't operate that way anymore," said Joe as he stood up and started to walk back to the beach. Golay slowly stood as well and wrapped his fingers around his gun. Joe stopped about the same distance he'd stood from Golay that night over forty years ago and turned around. Neither of them said anything for a couple of seconds. Then they drew their pistols and fired.

CHAPTER 25

WANDERING SOULS

Thornhill stood motionless in the train station as the morning rush of commuters passed by him, heading toward their trains, a few pausing to stand beside him to see what was going on. A police officer stood in front of a single-stall bathroom where the three girls Thornhill had met earlier lay naked on the bathroom floor, dead. Purple-and-black bruises covered their bodies as they lay on top of each other next to the toilet. Their throats were cut open, the blood already drying to create a crisp outer layer. The police started their routine: taping off the bathroom, taking pictures of the crime scene, and discussing the cause of death of the three girls. Once they had finished taking the pictures, two young officers picked up the bodies and placed them in three separate black body bags. The way these officers maneuvered the bodies indicated they had done this type of thing one too many times in their young lives. An older officer told onlookers to move along. Thornhill left before the officer reached him.

Thornhill somberly walked toward his track to wait for his train. After passing through security relatively easily—he had left his gun in a sewer drain he had passed on his way to the station—he had a couple of minutes before his departure time. He went to the train station's drugstore and bought the latest book in the Lion series with cash. He still reached his platform before his train, which was not good for his mind. His thoughts wandered to what would have happened if he had walked the girls to the train station. He knew, though, that if he had, he would have missed his chance meeting with Fredrick before he died. But what if? What if he had walked them to a cab, would that have changed anything? What if he hadn't even asked for the girls and had just tried another way to get what he needed from Fredrick? Thornhill soon lost all control of his thoughts. They spiraled him down to a dark place of doubt, depression, and guilt.

His train arrived and brought him back to the real world, jolting him from his dazed state. He boarded and sat in the back next to the window. As the train filled up, no one made their way to the seat next to him. Businessmen off to meetings and exchange students off to classes across town took most of the seats. The doors closed, and the train jolted out of the station, heading to its multiple stops before exiting the country where Thornhill would find a plane back home to shake off the paper trail. He felt his mind wander again toward depression as he wondered if he should have risked trying to find Jones instead of hoping he was all right, risked exposing himself to ease his conscience instead of sticking with the plan.

A small boy snapped Thornhill out of his thoughts. The boy sat in the empty seat beside him and put his blue-and-red backpack on his lap. He reminded Thornhill of the boy he'd seen at the airport at the beginning of his mission. The little boy watched the front of the train as if he was waiting for someone, then he glanced in Thornhill's direction and jumped a little, seemingly surprised that someone was sitting next to him, the same attitude Thornhill had, though without the physical movement. They stared at each other for a few seconds before the conductor came by to check their tickets. The conductor punched Thornhill's ticket, gave it back, and then held out an open hand to the little boy.

"His mother has his ticket. She's in another car talking to a friend," said Thornhill. The conductor gave a nod and went on punching tickets. By the time he reached the next car, he had obviously forgotten all about the little boy's ticket. When the conductor left the car, the boy looked at Thornhill. His bright-blue eyes said a soft thank you.

"Just promise me you have a good reason for running away," said Thornhill.

The boy gave him a questioning look.

"It's obvious," said Thornhill. "Clutching your backpack like there's no tomorrow. No ticket or pass on you. And you seem nervous, like you're going to be found out. So just promise me it's not stupid." Thornhill made sure his displeasure showed in his voice.

The boy looked down at his feet and gave a soft-spoken response. "It probably is. I guess they're right."

"What's your name?"

"Mathias. Yours?"

"Thomas. Who's right, Mathias?"

"Everyone."

Thornhill then did something that never happened to Mathias: he listened. He listened to this little boy with dark-brown hair and bright-blue eyes talk of his life, a life that started as a joke by some teenage boys who poked a needle through a couple of condoms at the gas station they worked at. Mathias's parents didn't know that when they did it in his grandfather's bathroom. Nine months later, Mathias came into this world of pain and suffering by the skin of his teeth and after the death of his closest guardian. A few months before he was born, his grandfather died without much to his name but with one request for his daughter, a last wish, really—don't have an abortion. She didn't, and she made sure her son knew that, telling him almost every day whenever he got underfoot. "If it wasn't for your grandfather…"

Mathias never met his father. Mathias lived in a house filled with a lot of smoke and needles. His mom had a lot of boyfriends. Some liked him and gave him things like stuffed animals or candy. Some didn't acknowledge him, taking no notice of his presence, talking over him when he spoke. Some hated him, throwing him against the wall, giving him a punch in the face if he spoke out of turn, or a firm grip on his lower parts under the table.

All this pain and hatred he knew before he was eight. This little boy of Amsterdam found his only comfort in books. When his mom would have parties or boyfriends over to do their things in the living room, he would hide himself in his room, locking himself away with his books and stuffed animals, reading about places far, far away where adventurers fought nature and beasts, where soldiers fought for freedom and country, where knights waged war against evil and injustice. In the books, he found safety...until he forgot to take the trash out. Then his mother beat him and cussed him out, screaming, "Get your head out of the clouds!"

Soon Mathias stopped reading fiction and started reading about languages. He spent every waking minute learning different languages, starting with English, since that is what his teacher said a lot of the world spoke. Christmastime came around, not a happy season for him. His mom got a Christmas card from his aunt. It was a family picture of her, her husband, and their two girls all dressed in white with their huge house behind them. His mom said nasty things about her sister. "The favored one. The one who went places. If I married a rich German twice my age, I would be twice as rich as she is!" His mom ripped the card in two and threw it into the trash. But Mathias waited until she left and retrieved the card from the trash can filled with broken glass and little bags with white dust in them. He taped the card back together. He rushed to his room before his mom could find out what he had done. He taped the card to the inside of an empty folder from school.

That was the day when he took charge of his life, the day he started to plan his escape. Over the next few months, he slowly built up his new file, getting road and train maps of Germany. He used the school computers to get the train times, destinations, and prices. He learned more English and a little German from his teacher, so he would know enough to get around. Once he had everything he needed, he planned out the day when he would leave, what train to get on, where to get off, what address to go to, and how much the trip would cost. He had everything set and ready. All he needed to do was to wait. Wait for the perfect day to escape. It wasn't long before he heard his mom planning a party for a bunch of friends. He knew from previous parties that the day after would be his best chance. As the day grew closer, he snuck some food to his room for the trip. However, he decided to wait until the day he was leaving to swipe the money he needed from his mom.

The day of the party was like any other day. Mathias went to school as usual, though at the end of the day, he gave his teacher a long hug. She was taken aback by this; he wasn't that big into hugs. When he got home, he locked himself in his room and waited some more. He hardly slept that night, partially due to the loud music but also due to his nerves. He went over every step in his head a thousand times: how he would get the money, how he would get to the train station, how to tell the cab driver in German the address, what he would say to his aunt, how he would say it. One step he couldn't plan or control but one he worried about often was whether they would accept him. These thoughts infested his mind until he fell into a restless, dreamless sleep.

His alarm went off as he finished packing. He hit the top of the alarm like always and zipped up his backpack, tightened his shoelaces, and left his room. He slipped into his mom's bedroom as she lay unconscious on her bed with two naked men. He slowly reached under her bed and pulled out a small, heart-shaped tin box. He left her room and went to the kitchen to open the box. The lid made a loud snap. His whole body froze as he watched the hallway. After a few moments of silence, he finished taking off the lid and counted the money. His alarm went off again, louder than before. He looked down the hallway. He had forgotten to turn his alarm off instead of putting it into snooze mode like normal. He heard bodies rustling. He grabbed all the money and ran out the door. He slowed to a walk only after getting several blocks from his house.

Walking to the train station, he found he was short about twenty euros. He took out his folder and went through it to see what he could cut. He came to the realization, when he reached the train station, that he would need to sneak onto the train. He followed the crowd through the station and made it past the security checks rather well. At least, so he thought. Looking at his plastic watch, he panicked, because he only had five minutes to reach his platform. He ran. He ducked and dodged through the crowd, moving as fast as his legs could carry him toward his train, checking his watch to see the minutes turning to seconds. Through the crowd, he saw his platform as the speakers in the station announced the departure of his train. He ran as fast as he'd ever run, determined not to let his freedom leave without him. As he came closer to the train, the doors started to close. With a great leap, he slid his little body through the closing doors.

CHAPTER 26

SIDETRACKED

"That's quite the story," said Thornhill. "So, what's the plan after this?"

"One more train and then a cab home."

Thornhill nodded. "Sounds like a plan."

For the next couple of hours, as the train raced toward Germany, they talked, though Mathias did most of the talking. Thornhill just listened and kept the conversation off himself. Once Mathias was all talked out, he took a nap, leaning on Thornhill's shoulder for support. Thornhill ignored it and read his book until a couple of minutes later, when Mathias took Thornhill's arm and wrapped it around himself like a blanket. Thornhill stopped reading and just stared at Mathias for a while as his mind retraced his own childhood.

Thornhill had been an only child, and hadn't had many friends because of the personal program his father had placed him in. He remembered the feelings he'd had as a child after a bad day. His father would pick him up, hold him close as he sat in his big, black chair, and just listen as Thornhill vented and cried his feelings out until he fell asleep in his dad's arms. He always felt safe when his father held him like that; he felt protected. Thornhill wondered if Mathias felt the same way now.

He took a deep breath as images of the three girls in the bathroom came to the front of his mind, thoughts of Jones bleeding on a hotel room floor, Golay meeting the tall man while Thornhill ran back home, the little boy at the airport. Thornhill wondered if it was worth it. He hoped it was worth it. He looked at Mathias again, and a feeling of dread came over him. This little boy had never met his aunt in person. He didn't know if she was a good person, a loving mother, or a spoiled gold digger, an abuser, a pervert.

The train slowed to halt as it pulled up to the platform in Osnabrück, Germany. Thornhill gently woke Mathias up. He drowsily stood and gathered his stuff, and they left the train together. Thornhill walked with him to a ticket station, where Mathias bought his own ticket after much resistance from Thornhill, who tried to purchase it for him. Once they had both bought their tickets, Thornhill walked Mathias to his platform. As they reached the platform and their conversation drew to a close, Thornhill thanked Mathias for the good company and wished him a safe trip, though he could hear his heart screaming at him to stay with Mathias, to follow him to his new home, to keep him safe.

Mathias said his good-byes and told Thornhill the address of his new home, asking him to visit when he was in town. Thornhill wrote it down on a piece of scrap paper and promised Mathias he would visit. As Mathias boarded the train, Thornhill slipped some euros into his bag. Mathias sat in his seat and waved to Thornhill with much enthusiasm as the train started to roll out of the station. Thornhill waved back, careful to keep a happy face on. Thornhill hoped he had done enough, that his actions would help Mathias get to a good family. He hoped and dreaded the thought of seeing Mathias again as he looked at the address, wondering if he had just told the truth or a lie.

Thinking about seeing the results of his actions sent shivers up his spine. These thoughts haunted Thornhill as he boarded the train for the last leg of his journey home. Hope of redeeming himself prevented him from throwing the address away. Guilt over the girls' murders washed around in the pit of his soul as the train jolted to a start. The seat next to him was empty, and he placed his bag on it and stretched out his legs over his bag. Resting his head against the window, he went to sleep, a restless sleep consisting of a dream of himself as a child lost in a tilted city, the buildings eyeing him and watching his every movement as he walked the empty streets in search of his home. He turned a corner in the haunted city to see the three girls standing at the end of the road, their backs to him. He quickened his pace, feeling the buildings turn as he passed them. Once he reached them, the three girls turned around, changing their appearance to body bags.

They fell on him. He quickly retreated, falling on his back and sliding far away from them as if there was no gravity resisting him. Before he knew it, the three bodies and the city had become a distant speck in space. He looked up to see a swirling galaxy flashing with lightning before it sent a bolt down to strike him and wake him from his nightmare.

His train had just pulled up to its platform. Thornhill gathered his items and left. He hailed a taxi to take him to the airport. It took him some time to get through security, as it does everyone, but he experienced zero difficulty. As he reached his departure gate, he tried to distance himself from his thoughts. He sat down in the gate's waiting room and read a little more of his book while keeping mindful of his surroundings.

Once his plane arrived, it didn't take long for him to board. Flying first class had its perks. The flight attendants went through the basic safety procedures. No one paid attention to them. Once he received his pulp-free orange juice, Thornhill settled in for his long flight. He observed the rest of the first-class passengers from his seat in the back of the plane. Boeing 747 first-class passengers are placed in the nose of the plane, while the cockpit sits above them. All the passengers just sat quietly, either reading books or on their laptops. It seemed more like a library than a first-class flight. Thornhill was pleased with this. Spies can get a lot of stuff done when people are focused on their own little worlds.

Thornhill brought out his bag and took out the papers Golay had given him. Being by himself, Thornhill was able to look over the papers objectively, without Golay trying to convince him he was telling the truth this time. It took a couple of hours to go through all the papers Golay had gathered, but once Thornhill had digested them, Golay's idea of an international underground organization looked like nothing more than that: an idea. The more Thornhill read, the more the idea shrank, and he started to believe this mission was a waste of time and of precious lives. But he kept thinking about what wasn't in the documents, what Golay had told him in person and advised him to never write down or type out, telling him that the light of knowledge could be the downfall of the multigenerational, international crime organization that had ruled the world from the shadows, that simply revealing the name was a risk.

CHAPTER 27

AN EMPTY CABIN IN AN EMPTY FOREST

The moon shone down on Thornhill through the Michigan trees as he approached a small cabin with a metal garage in the middle of an unnamed forest. The garage door opened automatically as he slowly drove closer to it. Once inside, one would think that the cabin had sat there for years, unattended and unused. Rusted tools hung on the walls with cobwebs and dust all around them. Thornhill rolled down his window and placed his hand on a dirty shelf that held a watering can and some pots. Nothing happened. Thornhill took this as odd. He assumed they could be doing some work on the elevator, so he retrieved a small flashlight with a knife hidden in it from the glove compartment and walked into the cabin.

The log cabin had a haunted feel to it. The wooden floor creaked under his steps as he walked through the kitchen to the living room. The only light source came from his flash-light and the moonlight beaming through the windows. He walked past the empty fireplace toward the coat closet in the hallway that led to the bedrooms. Opening the closet revealed an assortment of coats and scarves and a line of work boots on the floor. Thornhill awkwardly placed his feet in a pair of boots, the third from the right. They were an old pair of steel-toed construction boots, a dull-brown color, the kind people don't notice. Once his feet were secure, he quickly shifted his right foot forward and his left foot back. The floorboards under them moved the same way. He laughed at himself a bit, since that move always made him feel like an up-and-coming pop star. The back of the closet gave a quiet click. Thornhill placed his hands between a black leather jacket and a red plaid shirt. He slowly moved them aside, and the back of the closet slid apart and revealed the inside of an elevator, the same color as the wall that was concealing it.

Thornhill took his feet out of the boots and walked in. There were no buttons, just a small mirror about waist high on the right side of the elevator. Thornhill pressed his thumb against it. The doors slid shut, and the elevator jerked downward toward home base, just one of the many hidden entries and exits for agents of Glass. It wasn't too long before the elevator slowed to a stop, giving a quiet ding as the doors opened onto hell.

CHAPTER 28

CHARRED MEMORIES

Fire had burned everything. It had eaten away the front desk, leaving nothing but a thin, seared frame of charcoal. The fire had climbed the white walls, searching for more flammable things to consume in this concrete hole in the ground.

If Thornhill had been an average man, he might have panicked and not noticed the figure in a hazard suit at the end of the room with a flamethrower in its hands and a pistol on its hip. However, Thornhill was not an average man. He dashed to the front desk and hid behind it. He covered his mouth with his handkerchief to slow the invasion of the clouds of smoke into his lungs. With his other hand, he drew the knife out of the flashlight. He lightly tapped a hole through the burned desk. Looking through it, he saw the dull-silver pants of the mysterious figure's hazard suit and one arm hanging down, holding the flamethrower. Thornhill bent lower to look higher up at the figure and saw its other arm bent up to its head, activating its radio. Thornhill could faintly hear the muffled sound of a voice behind the flat hazard mask. The figure started to move away from the desk, heading toward the two hallways that split off from the room in the opposite directions.

Thornhill snuck around the desk, knife firmly in his right hand. The figure lowered its hand from the right side of its mask, and Thornhill made his move. Within two steps, he had slipped behind the figure, slowly slid the tip of the knife under the hazard mask—making sure not to harm the mask itself—and stabbed into the side of the figure's neck, and, extending his arm and flicking his wrist in a smooth motion, cut the person's throat. His other hand pulled the figure's head back, cracking what the knife had not cut. Thornhill pulled the mask from the dead body as it fell to its knees and then tumbled onto its face.

Thornhill placed the mask on his own head, took a deep breath, and then exhaled. He didn't have time to enjoy the fresh air for as long as he wanted to. He checked the hallways for any trouble, but all he could see was smoke and burned walls. Back at the front desk, he could see that the computer was burned beyond repair, giving him no hope of finding out what had happened in this once-safe place. He looked at the dead body on the ground. He nudged it over with a kick. The head lolled about. Blood poured out of the neck and oozed everywhere. Thornhill lifted up the front flap of the hazard mask and, with his handkerchief, checked for blood. It was clean.

Thornhill walked behind the body and started looking for a way to take the suit off. First, he pushed the decapitated head off the back. It made a small splash in the pool of blood. Next, he confiscated the flamethrower and its fuel tank. Feeling around the back of the suit for a zipper or Velcro, Thornhill came up empty handed. He flipped the body over. Blood rolled off the suit like a waterfall. Once the body was on its back, it took little time for Thornhill to find the zipper. He took the hazard suit off the body and discovered that the dead person was a man wearing bulletproof body armor. It was black, with no logos or insignias, separate parts covering different parts of the body with a hard outer shell like a medieval suit of armor. Thornhill surmised it was private military, and pretty new by the look of it, as well.

He searched for anything that could give him an answer about who the dead man was and why he was here. Nothing. This scared Thornhill even further. The suit was a little baggy on Thornhill once he had put it on over his gray suit, but wasn't too bad. If the invaders were private military, they would most likely not notice…hopefully. Hazard suit donned, Thornhill placed the flamethrower tank on his back and the new pistol in its holster. It was a model he had never seen, slick in design, shiny as new, with no wear or tear. When he had everything in place, he paused before leaving the reception area. Turning, he aimed the flamethrower at the body and set it ablaze. He then ventured down the left hallway toward Crumwell's office to find some answers.

The walls were covered in ash. He scraped his fingertips against the ash and burned plaster. It crumbled at his touch to reveal the hard cement wall behind it. Memories came to him of the first time he'd stepped into this base as a teenager. Crumwell had shown him the way around the labyrinth of hallways, which he could now maneuver through blindfolded. Thornhill's mind did not stay occupied with memories for long. He turned the corner to one of the many glass hallways of offices and meeting rooms, or what used to be offices and meeting rooms. A beautiful sight in its intact form, the whole hallway was lined with soundproof glass rooms that had been filled with white tables, computers, and employees in meetings with agency leaders or handling agents on the field. Now, in place of the employees stood almost a dozen men in the same hazard suits as the one Thornhill wore. Half of them were removing hard drives and RAM from the computers while the other half were burning everything they had already gone through and then putting out their own flames.

This little scene told Thornhill most of the things he needed to know about his intruders. This wasn't an inside job entirely, but they had to have money and some inside men to convince the fire department that this wasn't arson. And they didn't pull punches. Two other hazard suits walked in carrying a body dripping with blood and placed it on a burned table. Another hazard suit with a flamethrower came up and set the body ablaze.

Thornhill walked past it all, past the burned desks, past the burning bodies, past the intruders, all the while keeping his head up. Once he had passed them all, he took another two turns to end up where he had seen them retrieve one of the bodies. He stood in silence at the entrance of a long room with about a dozen dead handlers, secretaries, and analysts seated around a long blood-covered table to his right. To his left stood a solid rock wall. Fear almost engulfed him at that moment. It was the sight of Crumwell's office in lockdown mode that kept him from drowning in his fear. Thornhill rushed toward the large, square column in the far corner of the room. Reaching it, he turned to the rock wall, tapped on the door, took his mask off, and showed his face to the hidden camera in the wall.

He spoke softly. "Sir, are you in there? Please don't be dead, sir. Please don't be dead!" He continued to tap on the door, listening to the sound of flamethrowers spewing fire like mighty dragons. As he knocked, he felt the door slide aside. He pulled out his gun and aimed it through the open door. He slipped inside and ran up the one flight of stairs as the door shut behind him.

Crumwell's office seemed untouched by the chaos outside. His desk was cleared of all the papers and tablets he would normally have out when working. The pictures of his family had been taken down from his desk and cabinets. The black leather chair behind the glass desk was turned around. Thornhill aimed his pistol, safety off, at the chair. His finger was on the trigger, and he was ready to fire.

The chair turned around, and Thornhill clicked the safety back on and lowered his gun. Crumwell was sitting there, his old, thin hands resting in his lap with a small tablet on them, playing the security footage of the entire building. His eyes were red and wet from the tears he had shed.

Thornhill sat down in the black chair opposite Crumwell and asked, "Is Mallory OK?"

Crumwell dried his eyes. "I don't know, but we can't get sidetracked." He leaned forward and turned his tablet around, bringing up a map of the building. "You will need to stay in the…"

"What do you mean 'sidetracked'? We need to find her and get out of here!"

Crumwell shook his head. "We need to take care of this problem first."

"We can take care of this problem in a more secure location far from here." Thornhill leaned forward and grabbed Crumwell's shaking hands. "Was she working tonight?"

"Thornhill, you don't understand. This is probably our only chance."

"Only chance at what? Getting shot and cremated?" Thornhill threw Crumwell's hands back at him and stood up.

"Thornhill, if you'd just listen to me."

"No! You listen to me and tell me where my fiancée is!"

Crumwell leaned back in his chair, eyes and mouth wide open. Thornhill sat back down, falling into the chair like a ton of bricks. They both sighed.

"Why didn't you tell me?" asked Crumwell in a weak voice.

"Policy. 'Employees will not date or have sexual encounters with fellow employees.'" Thornhill knew Crumwell knew the rule well, since he was the one who had written it.

"I'm impressed by how you were able to keep it a secret among an industry of spies," Crumwell said. "I could have helped you if you'd been honest with me."

"Honest? OK, let's us be honest." Thornhill could feel his emotions get a second wind.

Crumwell leaned forward and glanced at his tablet. "The intruders are not heading toward our position or the vault, so it looks like we still have some time." Crumwell placed his hands on his desk. He started the stopwatch on his wristwatch. "For five minutes, let's be honest." He interlocked his fingers together, hands as still as stone, and he looked Thornhill dead in the eye. And for five minutes, Crumwell hid no secrets.

CHAPTER 29

Two Shots

Thornhill had a million questions but only five minutes, so he chose carefully. Handing Crumwell the documents Golay had given him, he asked if the intruders were connected to the group called The Twelve that Golay had spoken of.

"Yes. With the amount of money and power they have, it would be quite easy for them to come into a place like this and destroy any hard evidence against them and then frame it as a major accident. No questions asked by anyone."

"Then why haven't they been discovered, if they are that big?" asked Thornhill. He glanced at the tablet to see if the intruders were closing in on their position. Crumwell closed the file and placed it on the table.

"Because of stuff like that," said Crumwell, pointing to the file. "It's enough to arouse curiosity, but it's not enough to prove an international conspiracy." There was disappointment in his voice.

"Wait. That's not good enough?" Thornhill took a heavy breath and continued, his voice rising. "You mean you sent me on a mission to chase after a paranoid lunatic, leaving another agent stranded and possibly dead, simply to get some papers that are most likely worthless? Why would they go through all of this if it wasn't a real threat?" Thornhill was trying to find purpose among all the dead bodies.

Crumwell looked at him, waiting patiently for him to finish his rant, and then said, "They didn't come here for the papers, and I didn't send you for the papers. They came for Silence, and I sent you for a name." Crumwell looked at the tablet, frowning, worry evident in his eyes.

Thornhill remembered the name. "John Wu. Golay gave me the name John Wu, though I had never heard of him. But how did they discover our communication network? Isn't it supposed to be untraceable?" His voice had softened with curiosity.

"I believe they found Jones and discovered it from his cell phone or, heaven forbid, from him. But that is not what I'm worried about. I'm worried about what they might stumble upon if you don't stop them." Crumwell snatched up the files again and started to burn them.

Thornhill felt more in the dark than ever. "Stumble upon what?"

Crumwell spun the tablet toward Thornhill and enlarged the security screen so he could see four heavily armed intruders dressed in hazard suits heading down the hallway toward them.

"Your five minutes are up. Now listen. I don't know what happened to Mallory. She was working tonight on her own, so I truly don't know if she's all right. You will have to block that out of your mind now, because I need you to listen to the instructions I am going to give you very carefully and follow them to the letter." Crumwell pulled out two maps from his desk. "Remember where the vault is located?"

Thornhill nodded.

"Good. Within that room, in the back left corner, there is a hidden room. The tile on the floor with the chipped corner will let you in. Place your palm on it. It has fingerprint recognition. Inside, you'll find an emergency suitcase and backpack with everything you will need to get out. Above it will be a computer hooked up to a hidden server within the Silence servers in the vault. Turn it on, type in your name, and press the Delete button. There will be an emergency fire switch on your right. Do not pull it down as it says. Instead, pull it up. You will have less than a minute to get through the small escape door under the computer. Can you do that, Thornhill?"

Thornhill knew Crumwell was a man who didn't argue, who didn't debate, who gave orders to be followed without question. Thornhill nodded again, though he was still worried about Mallory.

"Good," said Crumwell. "Now, before you do all that, you must get past the intruders coming this way." Crumwell enlarged the security footage on the tablet again so Thornhill could get a better view. The four hazard suit–wearing figures, armed with advanced assault rifles, were walking down the hallway connecting the meeting room to Crumwell's office. "I knew they would overlook my office the first time through, but the second time, they will find us. You need to get to the vault. The only way that will be possible is if you impersonate one of them. You look the part."

Thornhill looked over his attire, feeling confident about the compliment. He looked back up to see Crumwell with a gun pointed in Thornhill's direction. Crumwell whispered, "But looking the part doesn't cut it. Most spies are found out not because they have the wrong attire or the wrong accent. It's because they don't play the part to the fullest."

All the confusion, all the worry, all the frustration, all the hurt within Thornhill stopped and was replaced with fear, fear of what Crumwell would say next.

"Thornhill," Crumwell said in solemn voice. "You need to shoot me. Right here." Crumwell placed his finger right in the middle of his forehead.

Thornhill slowly stood up. He could see, on the tablet, the intruders entering the meeting room below. Thornhill slowly pulled his pistol out of its holster. His eyes started to water no matter how hard he tried to hold back the tears. He remembered when he'd met Crumwell for the first time, so long ago. The intruders were looking around the table for anything they could have missed. Thornhill cocked the gun, mind racing for another way out, playing out a million scenarios of how to get them both out alive. He knew that wouldn't be possible. Crumwell raised his gun and aimed it just off to the side of Thornhill's head and fired.

Thornhill followed with a fatal shot.

CHAPTER 30

THE RABBIT HOLE

homas Thornhill played his part to perfection. He reported the shooting without a single quiver in his voice. Without hesitation, he opened the door so the other men could see the office and the body. He carried Crumwell down the stairs and placed him at the long table with the rest of the bodies without a misstep. He watched without moving a muscle as the room and the bodies were swallowed by fire. His eyes were not dry, though.

Then they found the vault.

The intruders were surprisingly quiet as Thornhill made his way to the vault with them. He suspected they didn't know each other personally or at all, which worked to his advantage. They walked through countless burned halls as they made their way down to the vault, countless burned bodies littering their way. None of the bodies bothered Thornhill as he walked with the invaders, though that quickly changed when they turned down Mallory's hallway. Thornhill didn't even recognize it until he passed an empty office with a couple of charred bodies lying outside it. It was an office like any of the others: a smoking desk with a busted computer on it, charred pictures of a family on the desk with a nameplate covered by ash, barely showing the name Mallory. Thornhill did not slow his pace, though his eyes did linger on that horrifying scene. Past the office, he looked onward as his heart beat faster. To say he didn't think about pulling his knife and cutting the intruders in front of him to bits would be a lie. Thornhill tightened his hands into fists. He knew he could take them on, and if he was quick enough, he could kill them all before they warned the others. He could feel his muscles tensing like a rubber band before it snapped. He thought about leaving one alive to drain off information, using old tactics that weren't the most effective but were the most brutal. His thoughts prevented him from keeping track of where they were going, and as they turned the last corner, they came to the vault.

Over twenty men in hazard suits were already there. They were waiting for three men to get the vault open. Thornhill consciously relaxed his muscles as he checked out the rest of the invaders. A majority had advanced assault rifles of a type he had never seen before, or they had flamethrowers. A couple had bags. He assumed they were the IT guys on this mission; the rest were protection and cleanup. Thornhill's heart rate slowed as he focused on the task at hand, his fists unclenching. Once the vault was open, a clear voice came over all the headsets. Thornhill knew this voice was not one from the group, because everyone stopped in their tracks, some placing their hands to their ears to hear better.

"Great job, men. This is a green room, so I want no harm to come to anything in it. We are now moving to the first step in the extraction phase. You know what to do."

Thornhill followed the flow of traffic as they all entered the vault in orderly fashion. Servers and cords filled the large room. Several vents punctuated the ceiling. The men with bags were at the front of the crowd and were handing out small black boxes, each with four cords coming out of one end. Thornhill saw a man with a black box slide the top off to reveal a touch screen and a touch pen inside. He then plugged the cords into four separate servers. Thornhill retrieved his black box and made his way to a row of servers near the left, walking past other men plugging in wires and typing on their touch screens. Thornhill weaved his way through the hallways made by the servers to the far left corner. There, he plugged in his black box and opened it up to see what it would do. A menu came up with only two options, upload or download. Thornhill suspected they were downloading the entire Silence program for later reconstruction.

He pushed his fear of what they could do with the Silence program to the back of his mind and checked the hallway. Only one other person was in it, near the front. He was looking closely at his little black box, as if it were a math test. Thornhill unplugged his black box and hid it in between two servers near his knees. He took out his knife and made a cut in his glove for his hand to slip through. He placed his bare hand on the warm floor tile with the chipped corner. Part of the wall slid back, revealing an opening big enough to crawl through. Thornhill checked his surroundings. The other man was still staring at his black box with his hand on his chin. Besides him, Thornhill couldn't see anyone else, so he crawled into the opening and ventured down the rabbit hole.

The room was barely big enough for Thornhill to stand in. The door closed behind him, leaving him in complete darkness except for a blue monitor button. Turning it on revealed the room, giving it a blue tint. The whole room was encased by the cement walls that surrounded the vault—a vault within a vault. To his right, at his elbow, was the emergency fire lever, looking like the ones found in hotels or supermarkets. On the floor, under the monitor and its keyboard, was a small black suitcase and backpack, simple in design. The monitor was mounted into the cement wall. Under the monitor was a floating shelf that held a black keyboard. Both monitor and keyboard looked cheap. A blue search bar took up the center of the black screen. Thornhill typed in his name and clicked the little magnifying glass.

Information flooded the screen with pictures, transcripts of phone conversations, e-mails, texts, purchase histories, Social Security numbers, everything. Anything and everything Thornhill had ever done was running past his eyes on a low-grade monitor. He knew that Glass monitored the majority of his activities, but the monitoring hadn't started with his employment or even with his training. He saw his birth certificate, his preschool attendance record, and his diplomas from all levels of education, even the letter he sent to Santa when he was child. It was all there, everything he had said or done, all of it, his whole life, compressed into millions of zeros and ones.

His eye then fell on the Delete button on the keyboard, seemingly no different than any of the other keys. Thornhill pressed it. A pop-up came on the screen, asking, "Are you sure?" He clicked the Yes button with some hesitation. The screen went black. Its backlight illuminated the room just enough for Thornhill to navigate around, but he stood still for a second, trying to figure out what he had done. What was he saying yes to? He felt that if he knew what the computer was asking, he would have pondered the question longer, possible even said no. But it was done.

He proceeded to phase two of his personal extraction plan as the men on the other side of the wall did the same. He slipped the backpack onto his back and picked up the suitcase. Placing his fingers under the fire lever, he lifted it up. It slid up smoothly until it hit the top of the little red box it sat in. Another small door opened up under the monitor and keyboard. Looking into the tunnel, Thornhill saw a flat wooden board on a rail that went deep into the darkness. He put the suitcase under him as he positioned his body on the board. Stretching his arms out like a superhero, he placed his hands on the hard cement walls that surround him and pushed himself forward. The board rolled with some difficulty but became easier to push as it gained momentum.

After a few seconds, he heard the door behind him close and then a similar sound farther away, followed by the faint sound of running water. He did not let this slow him down and continued to roll through the tunnel, stretching his arms even farther, pushing back even faster, fearing what might happen next, though nothing did.

He stayed in the tunnel for several hours, just rolling. He encountered small inclines and declines every so often. He continued to replay the events at the base over and over in his head: the man in the front office, the bodies, Crumwell, the bodies in front of Mallory's office. He hoped her body wasn't one of them. He put himself in Mallory's shoes, trying to think like her, playing out scenarios in which she would find a way out. The best one was her hiding and waiting for all the intruders to leave and then slipping through one of the many exits. He knew if she was there and if she had gotten out, she would head to her apartment.

Her salary supplied her with enough for a house of her own, but she had decided to save as much as she could for married life, hoping to quit Glass once they were married. She dreamed of becoming a mom and raising three or four kids under a safe roof, homeschooling her children for the first couple of years before sending them to the best and safest schools in the country, where they would start on their own great journeys. She had always wanted one of her children to become the president, or a Federal Reserve chairman or chairwoman. She wanted each kid to become someone great. She wanted to mother servant-leaders who would change the world for good. Thornhill felt his eyes tear up as he kept pushing, always pushing through the dark, grungy tunnel as he shed tears over all that he lost, over the loss of the present and the future, the loss of the good the invaders had stolen from the world, the loss of the children they might have stolen from him. He hoped with all his being that Mallory had escaped.

He saw a faint light at the end of the tunnel.

Reaching the end, he found a ladder leading upward. A small light bulb beside it illuminated the next tunnel. He climbed up for about four floors until he came to a steel hatch with a large wheel. Thornhill cranked it to the right and opened it to reveal the night sky. A full moon was low on the horizon, about to set to make room for the coming dawn. Thornhill observed his surroundings. Pine trees surrounded him, reaching high to the stars. The ground was littered with pine needles and bark. Thornhill took off the hazard mask to take a breath of the forest, to smell the peace of the night, to experience it for just a bit amid his chaos.

He climbed out of the hole with his suitcase and backpack and lay in a bed of pine needles in his cut-up, smoke-smelling, blood-covered hazard suit. He wept in the silence of the forest. He did not curse the world; he did not punch a tree or stomp his feet. He just wept. He wept until his body could not physically weep anymore. When he was done, he wiped his tears from his eyes and breathed in the peace of the forest once more as he stared at the night sky. Though he could feel his body finding rest, it would be years before his soul found any.

The silence of the forest was soon interrupted by the sound of an oncoming car filling the air with its manmade sound. To Thornhill's left, he saw headlights shining through the trees as the car passed him, headed off toward another pair of faint artificial lights. He rolled over, closed the steel hatch quietly, and covered the top of it with pine needles and dirt. He slowly approached the manmade lights. As he crawled closer to the edge of the forest, he gained perspective on his position. A two-lane road sliced through the middle of the forest. Down the road, Thornhill could see a stoplight where the forest thinned out to almost nothing besides the occasional tree here and there.

Thornhill took off his backpack and opened up its first compartment. A small pair of binoculars was inside, along with moist towelettes, a wallet, and some small hygiene products. Thornhill looked through the binoculars at the stoplight where the passing car had stopped. A bus stop sign stood beside the light with a small bench near it. Thornhill removed the hazard suit, opened the hatch back up, and threw the suit down the tunnel. He crossed the road and headed to the bus stop. Taking out a moist towelette, he was about to clean up himself a bit, but he stopped as he heard the sound of an oncoming bus. Looking behind him, he could see its faint light through the forest as it made the long turn around the bend. Thornhill wiped his face off as best he could and made a full-on sprint toward the sign. Reaching the bus stop, he sat down on the bench just as the bus came in view. He found a five-dollar bill in his pocket. With his left hand, he got his cash ready, keeping his right hand in his pocket since it was still covered in blood. He used the rest of the towelette to clean his shirt under his suit jacket, tapping it to pick up the loose ash. He stopped and placed the towelette in his pocket right as the bus arrived.

When Thornhill boarded the bus, the driver didn't give him a second look as he paid the fare. Thornhill took his seat. None of the passengers even glanced at him. They all had their earphones in and were looking at their phones, except for one older lady in the back who was reading a magazine about soap operas. Thornhill sat two seats behind the bus driver, backpack in his lap, suitcase at his feet. The bus rolled away from the bus stop as it headed toward the Rosa Parks Transit Center in Detroit.

CHAPTER 31

THE PERFECT SPY

And there he sat, in a stall at the transit center, his suit folded up in a plastic bag with the dirty moist towelettes and shoes, his khaki pants and V-neck shirt fitting him comfortably. The Walther PPK/S rested in his hands, cold to his touch. He sighed and closed up the suitcase of clothes. He opened up the backpack to see what was inside. The smallest compartment contained the personal hygiene items, binoculars, and small wallet. Opening up the wallet, Thornhill found eight different credit card gift cards (no more than two from the same company), ten thousand euros, and a key. The main compartment of the backpack held three large, empty envelopes with the same address. Undershirts and underwear took up most of the rest of the space, with six different passports under them, each with different names but all with his picture and description. Near the back, he found a file and an unaddressed envelope. Opening the envelope, he found a letter from Crumwell.

Dear Thomas,

I hope I was able to give you this file in person. If I did not, then I assume the worst. Here are the things you must know.

Inside this file is all the information I have collected about the criminal organization known only as The Twelve. Read it, memorize it, and then destroy it. If any of them catch you with it, they will either kill you on the spot or, worse, find out where you got it. I know it's not much, barely enough for a theory, but this is a compilation of the facts I've found and my own personal experience. With this and Golay's evidence, I hope it is enough to convince you of the horror from this hidden enemy, an enemy with many agents and powerful vassals everywhere.

The three envelopes are for mailing your gun in pieces to your apartment in Germany. There, you will take the information Golay told you and use it to find an entry point into The Twelve. This will be a long process and will most likely require you joining one of the most powerful crime syndicates and working your way up their ranks to even get a chance to see The Twelve. Have patience, an abundance of patience. Trust me. It took me a lifetime to achieve just four pages about them. However, the more I looked for them, the more I knew I was helpless to take them down from my position. That is where you come in. That is why I created Glass. That is why I pushed the new training model and made you the first subject of it. That is why I created Silence. Yes, it was a secure channel of communication, but what it hid was so much more. It hid the sponge. An Internet sponge absorbing every single bit of data on you, compiling it, and leaving strings to know where it came from, so with a simple click on Delete, you would effectively vanish from the face of the earth, making you the perfect spy, the perfect agent to infiltrate this hidden enemy.

A part of me hopes that you never read this, hopes that The Twelve is just a figment of the imaginations of two old men from a cold war era, and that all the preparation for this will be used to eliminate less dangerous evils. If it isn't, however, then I pray that you take up this journey I have entrusted to you, that you will find in you the passion to expose the truth and bring what was in the dark into the light. Many will oppose you. Some won't believe you. A lot won't care. That is the generation you were born into. That was the generation I was born into. Generation after generation of people have accepted the truth served to them by this corrupted organization because they are too lazy to search for the truth for themselves. But not you. I have given you the truth. I have pulled back the curtain, and now you have the chance to do that with the world: to pull back the curtain, expose the evildoers, and bring them to justice. However, it is your choice. Being where I am now, I can't tell you what to do. You are on your own. I know you will make the best choice for yourself. And remember: play the part. Good luck,

Crumwell

24207239R00096

Made in the USA
San Bernardino, CA
15 September 2015